Stay Away
from the Swamp

Look for these SpineChillers™

SPINE CHILLERS™

Stay Away
from the Swamp

Fred E. Katz

THOMAS NELSON PUBLISHERS
Nashville • London • Vancouver

Published in Nashville, Tennessee, by Tommy Nelson™, a division of NelsonWord Publishing Group, Thomas Nelson, Inc., Publishers, and distributed in Canada by Word Communications, Ltd., Richmond, British Columbia. SpineChillers™ is a trademark of Thomas Nelson, Inc., Publishers.

Scripture quoted from the *International Children's Bible, New Century Version,* copyright © 1983, 1986, 1988 by Word Publishing, Dallas, Texas 75039. Used by permission.

Editor: Lila Empson; Copyeditors: Cathy Norman Peterson, Nedra Lambert; Packaging: Sabra Smith.

ISBN 0–7852–7489–8

Printed in the United States of America.

1 2 3 4 5 6 — 01 00 99 98 97 96

1

"Hammer? Come on in here." Clint Gleeson set the pizza box on the snack bar. He opened the box. The aroma from the hot cheese, pepperoni, onions, and black olives made his mouth water. "Hey—Hammer?"

No answer.

Clint stood up straight. Though it was high noon on a July day, he felt a chill. It raised goose bumps on his arms.

Where was everybody? When had the house gone silent? It was as if his family, and his friend Eddie Hammer, had vanished.

"Hammer?" Clint called.

No response. A drip from the faucet plinked into the sink.

Just then a thin, high-pitched hum pierced the silence. Though not loud, it was a clear, continuous beam of sound. It seemed to penetrate Clint's eardrums, setting him on edge.

"Hammer!" Clint barked. "Quit fooling around!"

Still no answer. Just that continuous hum.

Clint glanced around the kitchen, then breathed a sigh of relief. He remembered now. The refrigerator had started humming that new, high note when the motor cut on. That probably meant the thing was going to break any day now. He scolded himself for feeling so jumpy.

Clint walked to the breakfast area and peered through the open doorway into the family room. "Hammer!" His voice cracked. "Come and get it!"

A slim, dark form crept out of the shadows.

Clint jumped.

"You feel it too, don't you?" the form whispered. "I can tell." The dark-haired figure in black clothes stepped into the light that flooded the breakfast room.

"Good grief, Hammer. Quit it! Let's eat." Clint's voice was loud.

"You feel it too." Hammer followed Clint to the kitchen. He looked nervously at the basement door. He checked under his stool before he sat down at the snack bar. "Go on. Admit it."

Ever since Clint and his family moved into their new home, Hammer had acted jumpy whenever he came over. He had told Clint that something about the house gave him the creeps.

It was true that when his parents bought the old

Lomer place it was run down and looked kind of spooky. But they had fixed it up. The rooms were light and airy now, with lots of new modern fixtures.

That didn't matter to Hammer. He was still scared of the house. And whenever Clint pushed him for details about what was frightening him, Hammer's responses were vague. "Something's just not right here," he would respond. "Can't you feel it?"

At first, Clint had been able to shrug off Hammer's suspicions and fears about the place. Lately, however, Hammer's fear had begun to rub off on Clint. But he wasn't ready to admit that to him.

"It's just you making me crazy." Clint tore a gooey wedge from his side of the pizza.

Clink, clink.

Hammer jumped a foot. The legs of his stool scuffed the floor. "Did you hear that? Something's in the basement," he whispered.

A rubbing, clinking sound glided up the basement stairs. Something rattled the doorknob. Whatever was on the other side seemed to have trouble gripping the knob.

Clint backed up against the kitchen counter. He looked at Hammer. His friend was white as a sheet.

The knob twisted. The door slowly swung open, with a low, creaking noise.

"Aahh!" cried Hammer. Clint felt his stomach drop.

"Hey, guys." Clint's dad poked his head into the

kitchen. He pulled the last three feet of garden hose after him. Rub, clink, rub, clink. The metal end knocked on the stairs.

"Whew." Breath rushed out of Hammer. "It's you." He frowned. "Hey, Mr. G? You . . . you are sure that's a hose?"

"Huh?" Mr. Gleeson wrinkled his brow. "What are you talking about?"

"Just . . ." Hammer licked his lips. "Are you sure there's nothing funny about that hose?"

Mr. Gleeson shrugged. "Plain old garden hose." He pinched a few of its coils. "Same one we had at the old house."

"Okay." Hammer smiled weakly. "But tell me something, Mr. G." The smile was gone now. "We didn't hear you walking up the stairs. How did you bring up the hose without making footsteps?"

"What?" Mr. Gleeson looked puzzled. "Of course I made footsteps. But when I got to the top, the hose unrolled." He shrugged. "Down it went. I just hauled it back up."

"While he was climbing the steps, I was trying to coax you out here." Clint pushed the pizza box toward Hammer. "Dig in."

"Well, okay." Hammer reached into the box. He smiled a real smile. "Hey, Mr. G, I can give you a great deal on a slice of pizza. Five toppings. $1.75." Hammer picked toppings from Clint's half of the pizza and put them on his own slice. Grinning, he held it out to Mr. Gleeson.

Clint's dad pulled a dollar and change out of his pocket. "You're not a bad sales rep."

"Going to hire me at your computer store?"

"We'll see when you get old enough." Mr. Gleeson smiled.

Mr. Gleeson set the coiled hose on the floor and joined the boys at the snack bar. "Speaking of deals." He wiped his lips on a napkin. "Clint, Mom and I made a decision. We're going to buy the property next door."

"Aarrgh!" Hammer gurgled through a mouthful of pizza.

Clint and his dad stared at him. They thought he was going to choke.

Hammer swallowed. His eyes were wild. "You're going to buy the Haunted Swamp?"

"I beg your pardon?" said Mr. Gleeson.

"Isn't living next door to the place bad enough?" Hammer shrieked. "No offense or anything. But don't you know what could be getting into your basement? And now you want to buy . . . *it*? Haunted Swamp?"

"Tell me what you're talking about." Clint's voice was shaky.

Clint had heard kids talk about Haunted Swamp. He'd never been sure where it was, though. He didn't want to appear dumb, so he'd never asked. Was Hammer saying it was the land next door?

"Snake ghosts slither through the reeds." Hammer made his voice spooky. His eyes opened to the size of headlights. "Twisty snake trails of flattened grass cover the land."

"Now, Hammer," Clint's dad said, placing a hand on his shoulder. "You surprise me with that kind of talk. I can tell you're really frightened. Are you, son?"

Hammer nodded nervously.

"Hmm. You mind handing me that duct tape? Thanks. Let me tell you something about fear. Sometimes it's healthy for you and sometimes it's not. Here, hold this." Mr. Gleeson pulled off a strip of tape, handed the roll to Hammer, and continued to talk as he wrapped up a leak in the hose.

"Healthy fear is, say, fear of being burned, so you don't touch the eye of the stove. Or you take precautions when you're using the lawn mower. Makes sense, right?"

Hammer nodded again. "Yes, sir."

"Then there's unhealthy fear," Mr. Gleeson continued. "That's being afraid of things you can't do anything about. Like thunder and lightning. Falling on the ice. And ghosts.

"Remember that Scripture we learned in Bible class? The one in Psalm 34? 'I asked the Lord for help, and he answered me. He saved me from all that

6

I feared.' I expect if you seek the Lord on this, he'll help you out.

"There, that ought to do it," he said as he pressed the last of the tape into place. "I hope you'll think about that verse, Hammer.

"Son," he asked, turning to Clint, "have you seen my pliers?"

"I think they're on the window box on the back porch," Clint answered.

"Thanks." He tousled Hammer's hair, then he tousled Clint's and was out the door in search of his pliers.

"I think your dad must know everything in the whole world," Hammer said.

"He is pretty neat, isn't he?" Clint said. If he did say so himself, he had the best father around. Even though work kept him pretty busy, he made time to coach Clint's Little League team and teach his Bible class at church.

"Who started that nonsense about Haunted Swamp anyway?" Clint wondered.

"Who knows? But no matter what your father says, I wouldn't go into Haunted Swamp for . . . even for a million dollars," Hammer declared.

Clint felt another chill race up his spine. Clearly, Hammer was frightened of the property next door. But what did he mean when he said something could be getting into the Gleesons' basement? Was

he saying that ghosts could invade the Gleesons'
home?

Suddenly Clint wasn't hungry anymore. He set his
slice of pizza on the plate and looked out the window at his dad, who was now busy with the pliers.

Clint shivered. Out of the corner of his eye he
saw something move on the kitchen floor—something that moved without making a sound.

Clint drew a deep breath and turned to look at the floor where he had spotted the movement. He stiffened when his glance fell on the coiled shape on the floor behind his dad's stool.

Almost immediately he exhaled and relaxed. Part of the garden hose had come uncoiled. That was all. Apparently his dad had coiled the old hose too tightly.

Clint glanced at Hammer. Fortunately, he hadn't noticed his nervousness. He also didn't notice him jump when his father slammed the screen door on the way back in.

"I'm going to remember what you said, Mr. G, but I thought you should know that land you want to buy is crawling with snake ghosts." Hammer gave Mr. Gleeson a worried look. "Maybe you better think about this some more."

"You said you wouldn't go there," said Mr. Gleeson.

"So how do you know there are trails flattened by these so-called snake ghosts?"

"The whole town knows!" Hammer's tone was shrill. "There's something creepy about that cabin on the property too. People who have dared to go into the swamp have reported seeing flashing lights through the cabin windows."

"Probably kids playing. And just to show you how gossip distorts the truth, you should know that the land isn't even swampy. Yet it's called . . . what was the name?"

"Haunted Swamp!"

"This may be Florida, but not all the land is swamp. I wouldn't buy a swamp," Mr. Gleeson pointed out.

Clint's dad swallowed a bite of pizza and reached for his car keys.

"I've got to check on things down at the store, guys. Enjoy the rest of your lunch. And don't forget to clear the counter before your mom gets home, Clint."

"Okay, Dad."

After Mr. Gleeson left for work, Clint couldn't get his mind off the land next door.

"Hammer, if you knew that overgrown property next door was Haunted Swamp, why didn't you tell me?"

"I thought you already knew," Hammer replied.

"What did you think I was talking about when I asked you if you felt anything strange going on around here?"

"I didn't know! You never came straight out and told me what you were afraid of. I thought maybe you were spooked by this old house."

"I am! I mean, because it's so close to the swamp."

"Hammer, you heard what Dad said. The stories about Haunted Swamp are just gossip."

"I wish I could believe that, Clint. But I can't shake the eerie feeling I get around this place.

"Hey, what time is it? I've got to get going. Do you want to come over to my house?"

"Okay . . . well, no, I can't. I've got a ball game later this afternoon. I've got to wait here on Mom."

"I'll call you later," Hammer said before shutting the front door behind him.

From the front window, Clint watched his friend pedal away on his bike. He went back to the kitchen and cleared off the snack bar. Then he walked into the family room.

Tall, wide windows stood on each side of the fireplace. Clint went to the one on the left and stared out at Haunted Swamp.

Next to the Gleesons' neatly mowed yard, the swamp reminded Clint of the messy kid's half of a shared bedroom. It was a jungle, bursting with green plant life. Long, thick vines hung like tentacles from the trees. Tangled grasses, like greedy arms, crowded the edge of the Gleesons' lawn. They looked as if they might yank up bits of his yard while no one was looking.

A breeze fluttered the leaves. A second gust sent the grasses swaying.

It was the wind doing that. Wasn't it?

Maybe not all of the snakes were ghosts. Clint had heard talk about real, live snakes in the grasses of Haunted Swamp.

Some of the kids said the snake ghosts used the real snakes to carry out their dirty work. The snakes slithered all over the property, creating so many trails that no one could ever get to know the lay of the land. Kids like him, creeping around in there, would get hopelessly lost.

At night the snakes could cross the property line, plowing the Gleesons' lawn up inch by inch, crawling closer, closer—

I'm getting as bad as Hammer! Clint clutched his head with both hands. *Lord,* he prayed, *please deliver me from all my fears. Thank you.*

He took a deep breath. Then he made himself stare at Haunted Swamp.

He examined every clump of grass and spray of leaves he could see from the window. Left to right. Right to left. Zigzag, up and down. He saw nothing out of the ordinary.

The place just looked overgrown with plant life, that's all.

Clint had just begun to relax and get his imagination under control, when *Wham!*

The garage door had banged shut. Someone, or something, was in the house.

Adrenaline surged through Clint's body. He looked around for something he could use to protect himself.

"Hi, Clinty!" His four-year-old sister, Kristin, bounded into the family room.

Even though there was an eight-year difference in their ages, people said Clint and Kristin looked remarkably alike. Both had inherited their father's blond hair, blue eyes, and freckles.

"I've told you, don't call me Clinty."

"I know a secret," said Kristin.

"Good for you."

"The Three Bears are real!" Kristin blurted out.

"That's nice," said Clint.

"They are! Goldilocks's Three Bears. I saw them. I know where they live."

"Where's that?" Clint asked, though he really wasn't interested.

"They live in the cabin," sang Kristin. "The cabin in the jungle place next to our house."

Clint swung around. His eyes locked on Kristin. She had his attention now. "Show me."

They clattered out the front door, Kristin in the lead. Suddenly their mom's voice cried out from upstairs.

"No, Clint! Don't leave the house!"

Clint jerked to a stop and looked up. His mother had yelled from the balcony off his parents' bedroom.

Mrs. Gleeson leaned over the railing. She was gripping it hard. Strands of reddish hair blew into her eyes. Her face crinkled with worry.

"What's wrong, Mom?" cried Clint. Had she seen something creepy from an upstairs window? Something in the swamp?

"Did you forget you have a game? I can't believe you haven't got your uniform on."

"Oohh." Clint gasped. He didn't know he'd been holding his breath. "I did forget."

"Well, you better get going. Kristin and I will walk over to the ballpark in a few minutes." Clint's mom went back in and shut the balcony doors.

Clint dashed up to his room. He pulled on his Little League uniform and grabbed his glove and cleats. Outside the house he put on his cleats and then raced to the ballpark.

Good thing we live so close, Clint thought.

Part of the ballpark also bordered Haunted Swamp. When his team was batting, Clint couldn't see the swamp. When he played first base, though, he could see it very well. And since the other team was so good, Clint had a lot of time to look at it.

From first base, Haunted Swamp looked huge.

From the family room window Clint had seen only a small part of it. But now that he was outdoors, he thought the swamp seemed to spread out for miles.

Grass and weeds grew so tall, Clint could not see the trunks of the trees. But the branches of the trees were visible, their foliage so lush that it covered the forest like a canopy. Clint imagined how dark it would be underneath those branches.

He saw only one clearing in the forest. Through this narrow path he could just make out the tiny cabin in the distance. It was the color of charred wood.

"Safe!"

"Get in the game, Clint!" yelled his coach.

Clint blushed. He should have got this guy out easily.

Clint's team lost, six to five. "So close," Clint moaned as he walked home. He was glad his dad hadn't been there to see his failure. No one had said they blamed him. Still, Clint thought his team could have won if he'd got a couple more outs.

That's it, Lord, he prayed. *Now I'm letting others down because of my fears. I can't let some stupid swamp throw my game. I'm going over there right after supper. I'll prove there are no ghosts in there.*

At home, Clint changed his clothes and ran down to the dining room. "Dad here?"

"No, it's Thursday. The store's open tonight," said Clint's mom.

Both Clint's mom and dad owned and operated the computer store. They took turns working shifts so that one of them could be home with the children.

Clint choked down two meatballs, three forkfuls of salad, and four swallows of milk. "May I be excused? I'm not very hungry."

Mrs. Gleeson excused him from the table, and Clint ran through the garage and out of the house. He looked toward the sun in the western sky. He would still have a couple more hours of daylight.

"Clinty! Wait for me," squeaked a high voice behind him.

"Kristin, you stay home," Clint said.

"I want to see the Three Bears. And I can tell you about them. Nobody else can."

"Oh, all right. Hurry up. And keep your voice down."

"The Three Bears are big," chattered Kristin.

They crossed onto the land next door. When Clint's shoes hit the thick, matted grass, he felt as though he was walking in slow motion. It was like walking in water.

Or maybe quicksand.

Clint grimaced. He stepped high. Grass blades flicked at his legs as he pushed his way through. He shivered at the thought of a snake ghost coiling around his ankles.

"The bears were sitting in their chairs," said Kristin. "But they didn't move at all. I think it was just time for sitting."

"Hold it." Clint stopped still. He thought he heard something.

Swish, sissss. There it was! A sound like something was crawling through the high grass. Or to be more exact, *slithering* through the grass.

Sssssssss.

Clint's heart skipped a beat.

Sss. Sss. Sss. The sound was growing fainter. Whatever was making the sound was getting farther away from them. Beads of sweat broke out on Clint's forehead and began to roll down his face.

"Come on!" Kristin said.

Clint gulped and started forward. He remembered something. "Kristin. Did you say chairs?"

"Yup. Chairs."

"In the cabin?"

"'Course, in the cabin."

"Did you play Goldilocks and go in?" *Keep talking, Clint*, he thought. *Forget snake ghosts.*

"'Course not. For Goldilocks to go in, they have to be not home."

"Where is the cabin, anyway?"

"Behind the jail tree." Kristin pointed.

Clint looked straight ahead. Masses of thick, twisted vines hung from the tree branches all the way to the ground. Clint thought there had to be at least a hundred of them. The vines did look like the bars of a jail.

Or like a hundred dangling snakes.

Clint winced at his last thought. He raised his gaze to the branches and leaves. They were so wide and thick a city could be built on top of them.

"Besides," Kristin said, "it was locked."

Clint's mind groped back to the conversation. "The cabin door was locked?"

"Yup."

Clint and Kristin curved around the jail tree. The land dipped down for a short while and then rose up again. They reached the top of a little hill.

Clint saw the cabin below. Kristin scampered right toward it. Clint, though, had trouble making his feet move.

Up close, the cabin looked like it had burned, yet it seemed sturdy. Clint shivered. How could wood look so charred yet remain so sturdy?

The cabin contrasted with the surroundings. It was the only thing made by human hands in that whole green mass of twisted vines. Who had lived here? And if this was an abandoned cabin, why was the door locked?

Clint watched Kristin jump up on a rock to look

in the window. He forced himself to walk down the hill.

When he reached the cabin he pressed his face to the dirty window too. He had no idea what he would see.

At that instant his concentration was broken by the piercing sound of his sister's shriek.

"Kristin!" Clint's right ear throbbed from the blast of Kristin's voice. "What? Why did you scream? What is it?"

Wildly, he checked for snakes clutching Kristin's arms, legs, or hair. He looked at the rock she stood on. Bare.

Clint jerked around and scanned the grass behind them. Nothing. But why would he have to see anything? Snake ghosts would be invisible! They could be anywhere. Clint tried to control his pumping lungs.

"It's really, really real," Kristin chattered. She still had her face pressed against the window, her nose pushed flat against the pane.

"What's real?" Clint spun back to the window. He rubbed his fists on the grimy glass. "I can't see a thing in there." Was Kristin just playing a game of pretend?

"That's 'cause they're gone," Kristin cried. "They

went for their walk. They even put their chairs away. The Three Bears are for real!"

Clint stared at his sister. Her pale blue eyes were as round as marbles. Her small cheeks were so flushed he couldn't see her freckles.

Kristin had to have seen something here. Something that looked like three bears. She wouldn't get this excited over a game of pretend.

"Moms and dads think the Three Bears are just make-believe." A happy smile bloomed on Kristin's face. "But they're not. They're real."

Clint peered hard through the window. He saw that there was another window straight across the cabin and one in the back wall. In the faint light he could see that the place was empty. At least there weren't any bears or chairs inside.

"Maybe it's 'chanted," sang Kristin.

"Chanted?" asked Clint. Through the window, he stared left, then right, as far as he could. He couldn't see a hint of color. The whole inside looked as sooty and dark as the outside. *What did she mean by chanted?*

"The whole jungle place is 'chanted. It's the 'chanted forest." Kristin's voice fell to a whisper. "Or else the bears couldn't go out of the cabin and walk in it."

Oh, the enchanted forest. Clint looked at Kristin once more. He was about to tell her she couldn't

22

possibly have seen the Three Bears, but he thought better of it. Why spoil her fun?

"Hey, Kristin, I'm going to look in the other window. You can come with me if you want. In fact—" Clint looked back at the tangled mass of green all around them. "Come anyway." Clint grabbed Kristin's arm and walked around to the back wall of the cabin.

This window was just as soiled as the first. It was dotted with water spots and larger splashes of dried mud. Clint cupped his hands around his eyes and gazed inside. He tried not to breathe the powdery dirt.

Again, the floors and walls looked gray, black, and shadowy. Going in there would be like stepping from day into night. Clint wondered if perhaps this was the ghosts' dark resting place. *Ugghhh.* He didn't want to think about that.

He was about to step back away from the window. But before he could move he caught sight of a shape hulking in a far corner of the cabin. His stomach lurched.

"You go away now, Clinty." Kristin yanked at Clint's elbow. "Goldilocks has to go in."

"What?" Clint shook her off his arm. Then what she had said dawned on him. He whirled to face her. "Hey, no way are you going in there. You stay here!"

Clint swallowed. He looked back at the shape. It

rose about a third of the way up the cabin wall. Though bulky all over, the shape was thinner on top than on the bottom. It didn't move.

Was it just the very darkest pocket of dark in the cabin? Was it the snake ghosts' sleeping cave? Was it—

"You go now, Clinty," Kristin pleaded. "There are no boys in the story. Goldilocks has to go in all by herself."

Clint remembered that Kristin said the cabin door was locked. He had no plans to try the door, though, or to let Kristin do it.

He jerked back from the window and looked all around its edges. He didn't think it opened. At least not from the outside. His stomach unclenched a bit. Kristin probably could not get inside the cabin.

"Clinty—"

"Sshh! Kristin, listen." Clint swung Kristin up on his shoulders. "Look in there. In the corner on the left. This is left." He wiggled Kristin's left arm. "Is that one of the Three Bears?"

Clint heard the gentle bump of Kristin's forehead against the glass. "That big lump? 'Course not. The bears are real bears. I saw them!"

Clint sighed. If Kristin wasn't frightened, then he certainly shouldn't be either.

An instant later his breath rushed in so hard he thought his chest would explode.

Something had crept up behind him. It curled around his ankles.

But it didn't feel like snake skin.

It felt like fur.

Clint screamed.

Clint couldn't bend his neck to look down at his feet. His neck strained backward as Kristin's weight sagged down, down, on his shoulders. The legs of Kristin's jeans rubbed hard on his skin.

Was the furry creature tugging Kristin backward?

"Clinty! Clinteeeey!"

Clint clung to Kristin's wrists. He staggered, fighting for balance. If he fell now, both he and Kristin would land right in the furry thing's clutches.

Or tumble straight down its throat.

Kristin locked her ankles around Clint's neck. With her shoes jammed against his jaw, Clint felt panic quiver through him.

But the fur was gone from his legs.

"Rrreeouw. Rrreeouw."

"Kristin!" Clint rasped. "What is that?" It certainly wasn't the roar of a bear.

"A kitty! It was a kitty. But it ran away. Clinty, I'm getting down. Keep holding my hands."

Kristin unhooked her feet from Clint's neck. Clint gulped a huge breath. He stooped and let Kristin's arms go. She dropped easily to the ground.

"A cat?" Clint asked. He fingered his neck gingerly. "Did you see it?"

"Sure. It was black with big yellow eyes. All black. But I can't think of a story with a black kitty in it."

A cat, Clint thought. A visible cat. A visible black cat. Not a ghost. But where had it come from?

"Hey, Kristin," Clint said, "you sure . . . you sure there wasn't something . . . pulling you off me?" He felt silly asking. He sounded as paranoid as Hammer.

Kristin cocked her head at him. "Pulling me? 'Course not. Nobody pulls on Goldilocks in the story."

Clint sighed. He supposed Kristin had just lost her balance. Maybe she had seen the cat coming and had twisted around to get a look at it.

In the dense forest Clint couldn't see the sun. But it must have been setting low in the western sky. The forest was getting darker. He didn't want to get lost in this place when the sun set.

"Come on, Kristin. We've got to go home. It's close to your bedtime." Clint leaned over to scoop Kristin into his arms.

"No!" Kristin screeched. She churned her arms and legs, trying to struggle free.

"Cut it out," Clint puffed. He reeled from her solid punches on his back. He winced as she kicked his shins. Still, he held on.

"You go home!" Kristin cried. "I'm Goldilocks, and I want to stay here."

Clint gasped. He almost dropped her as she continued to struggle against him. It was as if she was under a spell. She believed she really was Goldilocks! The ghosts had her under a spell!

"You're not in the storyyyyyy!" Kristin cried.

Clint was in no mood to be kicked again. "Fine!" He let go of his sister. He turned on his heel and stamped through the grass toward home.

If there are any snakes in my way, I'll crush them to dust, Clint thought. *I'll . . . I'll . . .* But he couldn't think what else he would do. His stomach churned with fear again.

What if the snake ghosts knew he was on his way to get his mom? They'd know Kristin was about to be rescued from them. And they'd blame him. Their fangs would rise from the reeds and—

Clint broke into a run, swishing loudly through the high grass. That way he'd never hear the snake sounds.

When he reached the jail tree he ran around it. He was afraid one of those long, twisted tentacles might grab him.

The ghosts had let Kristin into their story games. But not him. He was too old to play their games. They probably resented him for it, and they would get him. He was on their land.

Clint was pumping his legs and pulling in breaths as fast as he could. But he seemed to be getting nowhere.

Where was his yard? This grass that tugged at his shoes, the vines that yanked at his hair, they had to end sometime. Had the forest grown bigger?

Finally Clint saw his house. He lurched onto his own lawn. He dropped to his knees in relief. But the relief lasted only a second.

From behind the trunk of a palm tree, the black cat crept out. It stalked to the center of his yard, then turned to watch him. Its ribs rippled like a Slinky toy. Its gold eyes shone on him like lamps. It showed no fear.

The cat obviously isn't afraid of whatever's in there, Clint thought. *Does it know something I don't?*

He didn't have time to ponder his suspicions. Something was rustling the tall grass behind him. Clint sprang to his feet.

"Kristin!" he yelled. His voice cracked. "Kristin! Is that you?"

No answer. Just the continuing rustle of the grass.

The sound grew louder.

Clint looked at the tall grass bordering his yard.

29

Something was parting the grass—something low to the ground.

And it was moving straight toward him.

Clint turned and sprinted toward the house. When he was halfway to the front door, he stumbled and fell on the ground.

"Clinty!"

Gasping for breath, Clint looked in the direction the voice came from.

Kristin was standing at the edge of the Gleesons' yard. Her back was to the tall grass of Haunted Swamp.

For the first time Clint noticed that the grass towered over Kristin by almost a foot. It had been Kristin parting the grass as she ran toward their yard. Her body had been hidden by the tall grass.

Kristin walked over to Clint, who was still lying on the ground trying to catch his breath.

"Kristin . . . why didn't . . . you answer when I called?" Clint was so winded he could barely speak the words.

"Huh?" Kristin looked puzzled.

"Never mind." He was too tired to press her. He assumed she just didn't hear him.

"It got too dark, Clinty. I didn't want to play anymore."

So maybe Kristin hadn't been under a spell after all, Clint thought. *Maybe she was just caught up in her own imagination.*

The porch light came on. "What are you kids doing out there?" Mrs. Gleeson called from the door. She stepped out of the house and looked at Clint. "Clint, what's wrong? Why are you lying there panting?"

"We . . . were just . . . playing, Mom . . . I was . . . running . . . and I tripped . . . I'm okay."

"Kristin, it's about your bedtime. You better come in. After you wash your face and brush your teeth, I'll read you a bedtime story."

"I want to hear the story of Goldilocks and the Three Bears."

Clint groaned. He pulled himself up to standing.

As Clint and Kristin walked to the house, Kristin spotted the cat.

"Kitty!" Kristin exclaimed. "Here, kitty."

"Kristin, leave the cat alone!" In all the excitement, Clint had forgotten about the cat. "It might hurt you."

"Clint, it's just a cat," Mrs. Gleeson said. "And it's a very gentle one at that. I've seen it several times since we moved."

"Nice kitty." Kristin tenderly stroked the cat's back.

"You've seen this cat before?" Clint asked.

"Almost every morning when I walk out to get the paper. I think it belongs to a family down the road."

"Oh." Clint felt silly for thinking the cat was a messenger from the snake ghosts. So far, he hadn't done a good job taking his father's advice and overcoming his fears.

"Kristin, you can pet the kitty another time. Let's get you ready for bed," Mrs. Gleeson said.

Clint followed Kristin into the house. He headed straight for the telephone in the family room. He had to tell Hammer about his adventure.

"You went in there!" Hammer's voice was so loud that Clint had to move the telephone receiver away from his ear.

"I had to check it out, Hammer. I mean, if Mom and Dad are going to buy the place, well—"

"I can't believe it! Don't you realize the danger you put yourself in?"

"Don't you think you're overreacting, Hammer? I admit, it was pretty spooky. It's so dark in there. But Kristin thought the swamp was a great place to pretend."

"You took little Kristin with you?" Hammer cried.

"She had been in there before. Alone! She thinks

the Three Bears live in there. She even showed me to the cabin. That's where she thinks the bears live," Clint explained.

"Oh, man, you went to the cabin?" Hammer's voice leaped across the telephone line.

"Yeah. I even looked in the windows. It was pretty dark in there. There was something hulking in the corner of the cabin. Something big."

"What was it?"

"I don't know. It was too dark to tell. But Kristin saw it, and she wasn't afraid of it. In fact, Kristin thought we were in an enchanted forest. She was really acting strange for a while."

"Strange? What do you mean?"

"I mean she was so absorbed in her make-believe game. It kind of scared me. It was like she was under a spell."

"You could be right. I've heard stories about the snake ghosts putting spells on animals and even people. That's how they get them to carry out their orders."

Clint was silent for a minute. The thought of his sister being under the spell of the snake ghosts made him shiver.

Finally, he spoke. "Listen, Hammer. This has got to stop. It's one thing to be a little bit nervous, but it's something else to say my sister's under a spell. I can't imagine the Lord would be too happy with us for spreading rumors like that, especially when we've invited him into our hearts.

"Meet me here tomorrow morning. If something's threatening my sister, I've got to get to the bottom of it."

"What do you plan to do?"

"Just meet me here tomorrow. You and I are going in there together."

"Into Haunted Swamp? Listen, Gleeson, I'm your friend, but I . . . I don't think that's a good idea."

"Hammer, as you say, if there are snake ghosts and they're after Kristin, then it's only a matter of time . . ."

"Go on, Gleeson, I'm listening."

"It's only a matter of time before they come after me and my parents . . . and eventually the whole town. But if Dad's right, and the place isn't really a swamp and there aren't any snake ghosts, then we have nothing to be afraid of."

"I'm still not sure about this." Hammer paused. "But, okay, I'll be at your house tomorrow morning."

That night in bed, Clint had a heart-to-heart talk with his heavenly Father before drifting off to sleep.

"I really am going to have to count on you, God, to deliver me from my fears. Goodnight, Lord."

He hadn't been asleep long when something in the night jolted him awake. His eyelids flew open. His heart was beating rapidly. He sat up in bed and looked around the room.

What had awakened him?

A sudden flash of light momentarily illuminated the bedroom. Clint gasped.

In that momentary flash of light Clint saw a figure standing near the doorway of his room.

BOOM!

The sound of thunder seemed to shake the house. It sounded only seconds after the lightning flash.

At that moment something jumped onto Clint's bed.

Clint shrieked.

"I'm scared of the storm, Clinty!" Kristin wailed and grabbed Clint's arm.

Clint released a sigh. He realized he was trembling. "Me too," he managed to say. "That thunder is loud. But we're safe in the house."

"Clint!" Mrs. Gleeson called from the doorway. "Are you okay?"

"Yes, Mom. Sorry I screamed."

"Mommy, Mommy!" Kristin cried as she ran toward her mother.

"I know, sweetie. It's scary, isn't it?" Clint's mom stroked his sister's hair as she clung tightly to his mother's neck.

"Remember what I told you about thunder, honey?" she asked as she sat down on the end of Clint's bed, still holding Kristin close. "It's just God whispering."

"But he whispers so loud!" Kristin's voice was muffled in Mrs. Gleeson's gown.

"Yes, he does. You're right. And he sounds like he could hurt us, but he won't because he loves us."

Kristin peeked out questioningly.

"Yes, it's true. He loves you, Kristin, and I do too."

Another loud peal sounded from the sky.

"Somebody frightened by the storm, I see." Mr. Gleeson stood at the doorway. "Kristin, my girl, have you forgotten what thunder is?"

"God whispering!" his wife and both children answered, then laughed. Clint had heard that for as long as he could remember.

"Some friends and I were talking about thunder at school just the other day," Clint said. "We were repeating what our parents had told us it was.

"One girl said her parents told her God was moving furniture!"

Mr. and Mrs. Gleeson laughed, and Kristin again peeked out from the collar of her mother's gown.

"Someone else said it was supposed to be God bowling."

"I've heard that one too," Mr. Gleeson commented. "Your grandfather Gleeson always said the clouds were just bumping into each other. But I couldn't figure that one out. Clouds looked so soft and thunder sounded so hard!"

That drew an outright laugh from Kristin. "Clouds are so soft and thunder's so hard! You're funny, Daddy."

"Well, I'm glad you think so, princess," Mr. Gleeson said, swinging her up into his arms. "Do you also think you could get back to sleep? Kiss your brother goodnight. Morning will be here before you know it."

And it was. Clint must have dropped right off to sleep himself because next thing he knew sunlight was streaming through his bedroom window.

Hammer knocked on the Gleesons' door just as Clint was finishing breakfast.

"Hey. Some storm last night, huh?" Hammer sat down across from Clint at the breakfast table.

"I'll say. It sounded like it was right over the house."

"The ground's pretty soggy this morning."

Clint cleared his dishes from the table and took them to the dishwasher.

"Clint, I'm taking Kristin to day care," Mrs. Gleeson said. "Your dad will pick her up after lunch and bring her home."

"Okay, Mom. See you tonight."

39

"So what's the plan?" Hammer looked at Clint and wrinkled his brow.

"To find out the truth about Haunted Swamp. Come on. Let's get going."

Clint and Hammer walked to the edge of the Gleesons' yard.

"Is this where you and Kristin went in yesterday?" Hammer asked.

"This is it. Are you ready?"

"Clint, I don't know. Maybe we better think about this some more."

"Don't back out on me now, Hammer. I need your help in this."

Hammer looked directly into Clint's eyes. "You're my best friend, man. Okay. Here we go."

They stepped into the tall grass. The ground beneath their feet was soggy.

"This really is a swamp!" Hammer said.

"It wasn't like this yesterday. The rain really soaked the ground."

"The ground's not the only thing that's soaked. Look at my shoes." Hammer pointed to his feet. "Why do your parents want to buy this place anyway?"

"I don't know," Clint said, ducking under a low fan of leaves. "But if they do buy it, maybe they'll clear out some of this dense brush."

"Look. The grass is flat there, and there, and there." Hammer pointed as he spoke. "Just like everybody says."

Oh boy. Hammer would get going on snakes in no time. Clint didn't want to get spooked.

"Sure, parts of the grass are flattened," Clint said. "Kristin and I walked on it yesterday."

"Aagh!" Hammer screamed.

Clint jerked, then felt his legs go numb. "What is it?" Clint's voice was shrill from fear. "What's wrong?"

Hammer pointed straight ahead. "Look at that thing!"

He was pointing at the jail tree. "That's the jail tree," Clint said with relief in his voice. "That's what Kristin calls it."

"Look at all those vines!" Hammer halted about ten feet from the jail tree. "There must be hundreds of them. And look at the ones coiled around those branches." Hammer pointed. "They look like—"

"Like snakes," Clint said. "I know."

"Did you ever think maybe the snakes aren't invisible after all?" Hammer asked.

Clint didn't want to tell Hammer that he had.

Who knew what lived among those vines and branches? Surely snakes could. They could slither down those thick vines and coil around trespassers like Hammer and himself.

41

Clint looked up. The thick roof of leaves blotted out the sun.

Clint and Hammer wound their way around the tree. The vines hanging from the branches looked strong enough to swing on.

"You know, I saw an old Tarzan movie once on TV," Hammer said. "In the movie, he would swing from tree to tree on vines like these."

"I've seen some of those old movies too." Clint grabbed one of the vines and tugged on it. It held strong to the branch above. "Well, there's no reason why we can't have a little fun on this ghost-busting mission."

"What are you doing, Gleeson?" Hammer's voice was wary.

Gripping the vine with both hands, Clint backed up as far as the vine would let him. He ran full speed straight ahead and lifted his feet off the ground.

"Whoopeeeee!" Clint shouted as he swung on the vine into the air.

But his excitement quickly evaporated. The vine swung him higher than he had expected.

"Gleeson! Let go of the vine!" Hammer yelled.

The vine began to swing back in the opposite direction. Clint held on tightly. He was picking up speed. If he let go he could be seriously hurt.

Once again the vine was swinging him into the air in the opposite direction. To Clint, it no longer felt like a plant. It felt more like a long, strong muscle. It was toying with him, lifting him higher and higher.

Clint caught a glimpse of Hammer's face. It was panic-stricken. It told Clint that he was definitely in some kind of danger.

Maybe this isn't a vine after all, Clint thought.

"Let go, Gleeson!" Hammer shrieked.

When he began to swing back toward the ground Clint let go of the vine. He landed inside the jail tree's ring of vines. Say, this made a pretty good hiding place. If the swamp weren't so spooky, he wouldn't mind a hideaway like this.

"Man," Hammer puffed. He moved slowly toward Clint. "I thought you were done for. I thought one of the snake ghosts had taken control of the vine."

Hammer shuffled closer to Clint. He held out a hand. "Hey, Clint? You okay? You didn't break any bones, did you?"

"Nah," Clint croaked. He clasped Hammer's hand and hauled himself to his feet. He looked at his hands. They were covered with green plant stains. It was nothing but a vine after all.

Clint went back to the vine and gave it a push. It swayed gently. He forced strength into his voice. "A vine."

"What?" Hammer didn't catch what Clint said.

"Never mind. Check this place out, Hammer. It's kind of neat. You can almost hide in here."

Hammer looked around the dark enclosure of vines.

"I see what you mean. But I don't think it's neat. I think it's creepy. Come on, let's get to the cabin and get this over with."

"Hold it, Hammer! Look!"

"Yikes!" said Hammer when he saw Clint's discovery. The soft, mossy mound within the vines was only camouflage. Clint had found the snake ghosts' tunnel.

"Come on, let's go," Clint said, putting his hand to the entrance to the tunnel.

"What? Are you out of your mind? You can't go in there! And you certainly can't open the door. Do you want the snake ghosts to know we've discovered their passageway?"

What Hammer said made sense. He wasn't convinced they were dealing with ghosts yet, but he still could've caused some serious trouble by disturbing the tunnel. Whoever or whatever used this tunnel was best kept in the dark about their having found it.

"Where do you suppose it leads?" Clint wondered.

"My theory is that it leads all over town. Of course, it depends how far the ghosts have gone in their conquests."

"Maybe you're right, Hammer. But since when

do ghosts need tunnels to move around? They can go through hard surfaces and be invisible if they want," Clint observed.

"That may be true," Hammer said, "but don't forget ghosts have their early stages when they're still transforming. Plus, they need a place where they can drag their . . . victims."

They both shuddered. Suddenly the hideaway didn't seem so cozy after all.

"Come on, we've found what you were looking for, haven't we? Let's go," Hammer said.

"Not yet. This just raises more questions. The cabin is only a short way from here. Let's go." Clint rejoined his friend.

They walked through more clumps of weeds and grass.

"Cut around to the right," Clint said.

He hadn't meant to speak so softly . . . as if he were afraid something would hear him.

Clint and Hammer crept around the jail tree. Clint thought they'd never get to the other side. Was the jail tree spreading too? Just like the whole swamp seemed to be?

At last they made it to the top of the little hill. They peered down at the cabin.

The roof looked much steeper than Clint remembered. It seemed to point toward the sky. It made the cabin look like a ghostly rocket.

"Three Bears' house, huh?" Hammer's voice made Clint jump. "They must have painted it with coal tar."

"Let's go." Clint started down the hill before he could lose his nerve. Hammer stayed at his side.

"Here's the first window I looked in," Clint said. "Kristin claims she saw three bears sitting on chairs in here."

"What?" Hammer said. "You're kidding, right?"

They cupped their hands around their eyes and pressed their faces to the window. As before, Clint felt dust creep up his nose and settle in his throat. He stepped back from the window and sneezed.

That same instant Hammer let out a scream.

Hammer jumped away from the window. He almost knocked Clint over.

"What is it?" Clint yelled.

Hammer pointed to the window. "F-f-frogs!"

"What?" If he had heard Hammer correctly, he didn't know why his friend had gotten so frightened. Hammer had never been afraid of frogs before.

Clint leaned his forehead toward the window and peered inside. He saw why Hammer had been so shaken.

Frogs! The cabin floor was covered with them. Masses of them, leaping, jiggling, scrambling all over one another.

How could they just appear overnight? Had the rain caused this? There certainly weren't any frogs *outside* the cabin.

"Gleeson! Come on!" Hammer was already running away from the cabin.

Clint tore himself away from the cabin window.

The boys bolted up the hill. They stumbled and grabbed at green plants to pull themselves along. They flew around the jail tree.

Clint felt a stitch in his side. His lungs wheezed. How much farther would they have to run? It seemed that Haunted Swamp would never end.

Hammer was about ten paces behind Clint, when suddenly something snagged his left ankle. He fell forward and caught himself with his arms.

Whatever had snagged him pulled tight around his ankle. It didn't let go when Hammer tried to lift his foot. Hopping on his right foot, he looked down at his other ankle.

Hammer released a bloodcurdling scream.

"Snake!" he cried.

10

Clint turned around at the sound of his friend's scream. Fear constricted his chest, making it hard to breathe.

"Help me!" Hammer yelled. "A snake's got me!"

Hammer was panicking. Flailing his arms and screaming, he continued to pull against the grip on his ankle.

"I'll kill it!" Clint shouted as he neared his friend.

Clint reached into his front pocket and pulled out a pocketknife. He raced to his friend. Clint braced himself, then quickly knelt to the ground beside Hammer's leg. He drew back his arm to plunge the blade into the cylinder-shaped form wrapped around his friend's ankle.

That's when Clint got a close look at it. A rush of relief washed over him.

"Hammer, your ankle is caught in two loops of a tree root. It's not a snake."

Hammer was still panicking. It took a few seconds for him to grasp what Clint had said.

When he looked down at his ankle, he saw Clint steadily sawing away at the tree root with his pocket-knife.

"Just about got it. There. You're free." Clint stood up, folded the blade, and put the knife back into his pocket.

Hammer bent down and massaged his ankle with his hand. The root had rubbed the skin on his ankle when he had tried to struggle free.

Hammer's heart was still pounding. He took a deep breath of air. "I thought I was done for," he said.

"I know how you feel," Clint said. "When I was swinging on that vine earlier, I thought it was a snake," he admitted. "It's this place. It's creepy."

Hammer's ankle was sore. He was limping.

"I don't think I can run right now. You go ahead. I'll have to walk out of here."

"No way. If you have to walk, then I'll walk too."

The two friends walked among the tall grasses. Something was bothering Clint.

"You know, I don't understand how those frogs got in the cabin. They weren't there yesterday."

"When you looked in the cabin yesterday," Hammer said, "did you see the floor? I mean, clearly?"

Clint thought for a second. "No. It was too dark. I could just make out shadows."

"Do you suppose there's a big hole in the floor?

Maybe the tunnel leads there. Maybe the frogs get in and out that way."

"I suppose that could be," Clint said. "That would be an explanation."

Hammer stopped walking. "Don't you know what a hole in the cabin floor means?"

"No. What?" Clint stopped and looked at his friend.

"Where do ghosts come from anyway?"

Clint was starting to get the idea.

Hammer continued. "They come from . . . from the ground where animals are buried." He started walking again. His ankle felt better now. "So they have to come out of a hole in the earth. That's why they have their house right on top of it. And the tunnel you found is part of their network."

"Aw, Hammer, that's got to be the most redicu—"

Sssssss. The sound came from behind them.

"What was that?" Hammer cried.

Sssssssss.

"Run!" screamed Clint.

Clint's heart pounded. It had to be a snake. And it must be close.

"Heeheehee, hehheh, hawhawhaw." The new sound echoed behind them. It was a high-pitched, chilling laugh.

Not a snake. That was not a snake. Not an animal. Clint's thoughts raced. *It was either a human, or a—*

Ghost!

Grass, grass, and more grass. Where was his front yard? Clint began to believe that he and Hammer would never get out of Haunted Swamp. They would be trapped in here with the snake ghosts!

"Your house!" Hammer yelled. "Up ahead."

Clint and Hammer broke through the long grass. They broad-jumped onto Clint's lawn. They lay trembling and gasping.

They felt as if they had leaped onto a lifeboat. One that had been drifting away from them. It was several minutes before either of them spoke.

"You've got to tell your parents about what we saw and heard." Hammer's voice was weak. "I mean, I'm not going there again, so I'm okay. But for your own sake, man. And Kristin's. They've got to believe you."

Clint shook his head. "They must have walked all over that property before they decided to buy it. They must not have seen or heard anything unusual. They might think I'm imagining things.

"But those frogs, the tunnel, that horrible laugh—yes, now we know that some*thing* or some*one* is in the Haunted Swamp."

"Hey, Clint," Hammer whispered. "Look what's coming."

Clint lifted his head.

Kristin was coming toward them. She was wearing

one of her long play dresses. It was white and trailed on the ground. Her blonde hair was brushed out loose. A gold, glittery circle sat on her head like a crown.

The strangest thing was the way she was walking. So slowly, like she was in a trance.

She was headed toward the swamp.

"Kristin?" Clint heard the catch in his voice. "Where are you going?"

"They called me."

"Huh? Who called you?"

Kristin turned to face him. "The bears in the forest. They need me. They called me. Didn't you hear them?"

She turned and walked into the swamp.

11

Clint had to go back in there.

He didn't want to.

But he had to. He had to rescue his sister.

He rushed into the grass. "Kristin!" he yelled.

They wanted to get her. The ghosts wanted her. Maybe they didn't want him so badly, or they'd have taken him by now. Maybe that meant he could risk trying to save her.

"Kristin!"

He caught sight of her white dress. The skirt was caught on spears of grass.

Clint lunged for her.

Color rose in Kristin's face. Her forehead creased with anger.

She jammed her hands on her hips. "You spoiled it!" She stamped her foot. "Boys are not in the story!" She stomped back toward the house.

Clint felt shaken. Kristin had never been so angry at him.

"Good show, man," Hammer croaked as Clint crept out of the swamp. Hammer still lay sprawled on the ground.

"I thought there was a spell on her." Clint stared toward the house.

"Probably was. You broke it. Good show."

Clint shook his head. It was time he got hold of himself. "We've got to be imagining things, Hammer."

"What about the hissing noise? What about the laugh?"

"Kids," Clint said. He still stared toward the house. "Just passing through. Goofing around."

He looked at Hammer. "Hey, it's probably kids from our class. They're probably falling all over each other laughing at how they scared us."

"I don't know, man." Hammer got to his feet and walked to his bike. "For your sake, I hope you're right. But remember one thing. Those frogs we saw were real. So was the tunnel."

As he watched Hammer pedal down the street, Clint's stomach growled. He hadn't realized how hungry he was.

He went inside the house. His dad was home now.

"It's not quite lunchtime yet," Clint's dad told him. "Kristin's playing in her room.

"Will you do me a favor? Go down to the basement. In the storage area under the dining room, there are a bunch of shelves. Somewhere there's a can of WD–40. See if you can find it, okay? I want to oil the squeaky hinge on the basement door."

"Sure, Dad."

Clint opened the basement door. Creeeak.

"See what I mean?" Mr. Gleeson said.

Clint looked down the basement steps. It was like looking down a black tunnel. It was so much darker than the sunny kitchen.

Clint started down the steps.

They were steep. His shoes clumped loudly. About halfway down he smelled a damp, musty odor. He reached the concrete floor. Where was the light switch?

Clint ran his fingers over the chilly wall. A sharp needle of pain pricked under his nail.

"Ouch!" Something had bit his finger!

Clint felt along the wall. No. Nothing had bit him. It was a very rough, jagged piece of wall that had skinned his finger.

Where's the light switch? He opened his mouth to call to his dad. Then he heard his footsteps overhead, walking away. He had left the kitchen. He wouldn't hear Clint call.

Let's see. He had to go under the dining room. That meant he should turn right at the bottom of the steps. Then straight back to the corner.

Clint turned right. Cobwebs brushed his face. An

insect dropped onto his hand and scurried across his arm. He flinched and brushed it away.

He had gone no more than two steps when a rushing, whirring sound began. Clint gasped. Air began to blow.

A string bounced off his forehead. Clint grabbed it with both hands and pulled. There was a scraping sound, and the light came on. The chain clinked against the bulb.

Clint looked behind him. The whirring sound came from the dehumidifier. His mom had plugged it in to make the basement less damp. Its motor hummed. Water plinked into its tray.

Clint turned and squared his shoulders. The storage room wasn't far ahead.

As he walked, he saw how rough the gray ceiling was. It looked like gobs of rumpled tissue. Dust danced in the light. His sneeze exploded in his ears.

He entered the storage room. He needed another light. He couldn't make out the hulking objects on the shelves.

Clint scanned the ceiling. A pipe ran across it and curved down to two old washtubs. It must have been a plumbing pipe. And, yes, a small pear shape hung down from the center of the ceiling. Clint groped for the chain that would turn the light on.

Click. Light flooded the storage room.

Part of a long, cylindrical object hung down from one of the shelves.

As Clint stared at the form it slowly moved onto the shelf and disappeared behind a box.

Clint's mouth went dry. His heart thudded against his chest.

He tried to yell but he was breathing too rapidly. Finally he inhaled a deep breath of air.

"Snake!" Clint screamed.

12

Hammer's suspicions had been confirmed.

There was a snake in the Gleesons' basement.

The snake was as green as the grass in Haunted Swamp.

Clint knew what was happening. Haunted Swamp was closing in on his house.

The knobby head of the snake poked around the box.

Clint stepped back.

"Clint?" The basement door opened overhead. "What's wrong? I thought I heard you scream."

"Dad!" Clint screeched. "There's a snake down here. In the storage room. On the shelf. Come now!"

"A what?"

Clint ran from the storage room to the foot of the basement steps. He yelled to his dad.

"A snake! I mean it. Really. Hurry up!" *Before it hides in some hole,* Clint thought. *Before it goes poof. Before it changes into a green garden hose.*

Mr. Gleeson hurried down the steps, then he and Clint ran to the storage room.

No! Clint's stomach lurched.

It was gone.

Clint understood. The ghosts weren't going to let adults see them.

"Where, Clint?" His dad was scanning the room.

"It was behind that box!" Clint pointed to the box on the shelf.

"I don't see anything, Son. Are you sure what you saw was a snake?"

"I'm sure, Dad. It was definitely a snake." Clint's voice was trembling.

Mr. Gleeson stroked his chin with his hand. "I don't know how to handle snakes. Let's go back upstairs and call Mr. Rodriguez at the nature center."

"What for?" Clint couldn't understand how his dad could remain so calm.

"If he can locate the snake in here he'll be able to identify what kind of snake it is. He can take the snake back to the nature center, or he'll know the best place to let it go."

"What if Mr. Rodriguez can't come right away? Do we just let it crawl around in here?" Clint shivered. No way was he going to sleep in a house inhabited by a snake—or worse, a snake ghost!

"I don't see why he couldn't come today. Besides,

I'm not very comfortable having a snake in my basement. I just hope it hasn't started a family down here." Mr. Gleeson looked up at the shelves. "Hey, there's the WD–40."

Mr. Gleeson took the can of oil off the shelf and walked back toward the basement steps. "Come on, Clint. Let's call Mr. Rodriguez. Then we can have some lunch."

While Clint's dad climbed the steps to the kitchen, Clint lagged behind.

He surveyed the shelf where he had seen the snake. The snake was still hiding.

Clint grabbed the string for the light switch. He was about to pull it and turn off the light when out of the corner of his eye he saw movement.

He turned his head in that direction.

Clint stifled a scream.

The snake was moving from the shelf onto the water pipe.

Clint felt as though he were a statue. He was frozen in place by fear.

The snake's head poked forward as its neck swayed. Its tongue began to flick. Again and again. The tongue was red and forked.

Clint knew snakes used their tongues to smell. They could sense whether small, warm animals were nearby. When they found one, they would swallow it whole.

Flick, flick, whipped the tongue.

The snake inched forward silently.

Clint managed to step back. The dehumidifier droned behind him. Its sound filled Clint's head.

Whir, plink, whir, plink.

Hmmmm, the dehumidifier hummed.

Silently, the snake crawled forward.

Clint knew he was a goner.

13

Clint backed up. He jerked his head to look behind him.

Don't stumble and fall, he told himself. *The snake will drop on you then. And the ghost will fix you for trying to get it kicked out of the basement. It means to be king down here. And you're in the way.*

At that thought, Clint sprang into motion. He dashed out of the storage room and raced up the steps two at a time.

He bolted through the door to the kitchen and slammed it behind him.

The aroma of spaghetti sauce and garlic bread filled the kitchen. Spaghetti was one of Clint's favorites, but he had no appetite now.

Mr. Gleeson walked into the kitchen. "I just talked to Mr. Rodriguez. I got him on his car phone. He's on his way over."

He can't get here soon enough, Clint thought.

*　　*　　*

When Mr. Rodriguez arrived he was carrying a burlap sack. He told Clint that after capturing the snake he would use the sack to transport it back to the nature center.

Mr. Gleeson took Mr. Rodriguez to the storage room and pointed to the area where Clint had seen the snake.

Upstairs at the snack bar, Clint restlessly pushed his lunch around on his plate with a fork. He still had no appetite. Not as long as that snake was in the basement.

Clint jumped off the stool when he heard his dad and Mr. Rodriguez climbing the steps.

Mr. Rodriguez entered the kitchen first, clutching the burlap bag.

"We got him, Clint." Mr. Rodriguez grinned. "It's just a harmless green snake."

Harmless? Clint thought. Obviously Mr. Rodriguez wasn't familiar with the property next to the Gleesons' house.

"It's a common snake in this region," he continued. "They're nonpoisonous."

"Hector, would you care to stay and have lunch with us?" Mr. Gleeson extended the invitation to Mr. Rodriguez.

"Thank you, but I better get this little fella back to the nature center. We'll let him go in the grass around there."

Clint followed Mr. Rodriguez outside. He watched the man start up his car and drive down the street.

For a car with a ghost in it, it went down the street just fine, Clint thought. It didn't suddenly speed up, veer sideways, or hit a tree. It didn't burst into a ball of flames. It didn't disappear with a poof in a cloud of smoke.

Maybe the snake *was* just a plain, harmless green snake.

Clint went back inside to eat his lunch.

After lunch, Clint called Hammer and told him about the discovery and capture of the green snake in the basement.

"Mr. Rodriguez took it back to the nature center?" Hammer asked.

"He said the snake was harmless. That he'd let it go in the grass around the nature center," Clint explained.

"Let it go! Around the nature center? Where families and schoolkids go to picnic, fish, and hike? You're kidding me!"

"Hammer! It's a harmless snake!"

Clint realized his mistake as soon as the words were out of his mouth. Hammer would really get carried away with this.

"What makes you so sure it was a harmless snake?" Hammer demanded. "It won't be a harmless snake if a ghost has gotten hold of it and put it under a spell."

"So now the nature center has just got its first ghost. Is that what you're trying to tell me? What do you propose we do?"

"What does it matter?" Hammer chattered. "They're out of the swamp. They can go anywhere now. They can spread all over the world."

Hammer paused before speaking again. "This is serious. Meet me in your front yard. I'm on my way. We've got to think this through."

When Hammer arrived at the Gleesons', he and Clint sat down on the front lawn.

Hammer looked at the lawn behind and to their left. "I've got to tell you, I'm getting the willies just sitting on this grass."

Clint glanced down at the innocent-looking blades of grass.

"If the snake ghosts were able to get into your basement, then they can easily invade your lawn," Hammer continued.

Clint and Hammer jumped up and ran to the concrete driveway.

"If we can't trust the lawn, what then?" Hammer asked. "Forget bushes."

"And garages."

"And basements. Pipes, rafters, rain gutters—"

"And garden hoses. Hammer, we can't live like this."

"You can say that again."

"Get your bike."

Hammer's bike was leaning against the front porch. He didn't have to step off of the concrete to get it.

Clint warily walked into the garage where he had left his bike.

Looking around the garage, he got nervous. There were so many places where snakes could hide. Like in back of metal shelves. Behind paint cans. Under the edges of lawn mowers. Tucked among coils of rope—or garden hose.

Clint's bike was parked on the right side of the garage, against the wall opposite the door that led into the house. His dad's car stood between him and the door.

"You see something, Gleeson?" Hammer called. He was now standing beside his bike right outside the garage.

Go get your stupid bike, Clint ordered himself. Yet with every footstep, goose bumps broke out on his arms and legs.

He scanned the walls. They were smooth and white. Nothing could hide there.

He scanned the rafters. Lots of rafters.

All of a sudden the hair on the back of his neck

stood up. Behind him! What was that on the rafters behind him?

"Look out!" Hammer yelped. "Behind you! Up there! Thick and black! It's coming down.

"Run, Gleeson. Run!"

14

Clint screamed and lunged farther into the garage.

He leaped in front of his dad's car and crouched there. He hoped the car would protect him. He would hear the snake when it dropped, *thunk,* onto the car's roof. Or its trunk.

Please, not onto the hood.

He began to duckwalk to his right. The floor was gritty beneath his feet. He skidded. His eyes were even with the headlights. He only had to scoot around to the driver's door. Then it was a straight shot to the house.

"Where?" Clint shrieked to Hammer. He wondered how the snake would react to his shouting. "Where is it now?"

"Hanging down! A whole loop of it. Thick as a python. Black as—"

Clint made it around the front tire. "Black as what?" he yelled.

No answer.

"Hammer!" Had the snake landed on Hammer and squeezed him to death?

"Clint," came Hammer's voice. "Get up."

"What? Are you okay?"

"Clint." Hammer's voice was sheepish. "Get up."

Slowly, Clint stood. He kept his knees bent in case he had to duck down again. He met Hammer's eyes. Hammer pointed at the ceiling.

Stored on top of the rafters were two black inner tubes. One hung down far enough that Hammer could see it from the driveway.

Clint stared at the inner tubes. He released a long exhale, then straightened all the way up. "Hammer, I think our imaginations are out of control."

Clint ran his fingers through his hair, then continued. "Let's get a grip and think about what's happened. A green snake was taken from our basement to the nature center—"

"And if it was a ghost, the world is doomed," Hammer interrupted.

"Hammer, we have no evidence that ghosts live in the swamp, much less that any ghosts have come out of there."

"So you don't think there are ghosts in the garage?" Hammer said.

"No, Hammer," Clint said. "And they're not in the lawn and they're not in the basement. It's all been in our imaginations."

"Those frogs were real."

Clint knew Hammer had a point there. But he didn't want to think about it.

"I don't want to talk about it anymore." Clint's voice was firm. "And we stay out of the swamp!"

"We leave it alone. It leaves us alone," agreed Hammer.

The boys walked around the house to the backyard terrace.

Hammer sprawled in the porch swing. "I admit I feel better now."

"Yeah. We don't have to be afraid of the grass and the bushes. It's all in our imaginations." Clint lay back in a lawn chair. He tried to feel confident. But deep inside, fear and uncertainty gnawed at him.

"Feel that breeze, man." Hammer sniffed loudly. "Aaahh. Somebody's cooking on the grill."

Clint leaned his head back and gazed at the sky. It was as deep a blue as he'd ever seen. Huge white clouds drifted across it like proud ships. Palm leaves rattled pleasantly in the breeze.

"Take a look at that swamp grass." Hammer's voice was mellow. "Blowing every which way. Probably a bunch of ghosts stirring it up."

"Hammer, don't start on that again," said Clint.

"You're right. Sorry." Hammer's eyes closed. "I sure could go for a can of soda."

"Say no more." Clint got up. He turned to slide open the glass doors that led to the breakfast room.

That was when his eyes caught sight of a white-robed figure at the far edge of Haunted Swamp.

15

In a twinkling, the grass parted. The white figure stepped through and was swallowed up. It was a part of the swamp Clint had never explored before.

"Hammer!" Clint's voice was sharp.

"Huh?" Hammer snorted as if waking up. "What did I do?"

"Did you see—" Clint stared at the spot where he'd seen the white-robed figure vanish. "No. Of course you didn't see."

"See what?" Hammer was alert now. The swing creaked loudly as Hammer jumped out of it to stand beside Clint.

"Even I'm not sure I saw it."

"Did you see it in the swamp?" Hammer asked. "If you saw it in the swamp, it doesn't matter how weird it was. In the swamp, anything goes. That's our new motto. And we're staying out of the swamp. For good.

"So what was it? Lay it on me, man." Hammer clapped Clint's shoulder.

"It was white and . . . billowy. The swamp grass swallowed it up. It was—"

"An angel?" Hammer asked doubtfully.

"I wonder . . . I just wonder," Clint said. "Could that be how God is going to help us fight this thing? He's going to send his angels? Think about it. When Shadrach, Meshach, and Abednego went into the fiery furnace, they didn't go alone. We may not be in a fiery furnace, but we're certainly in the hot seat.

"Unless . . . oh, man." Clint whirled and shoved the sliding door aside. He dashed through the breakfast room, down the hall, to the foyer. He pounded up the stairs and burst into Kristin's room.

She wasn't there.

Clint looked under the bed. He found nothing except dust and two Barbie dolls.

He slid open her closet door. He ran his hands through the dresses, shirts, and pants. She wasn't hiding there either.

He checked the bathroom, his own room, and even his parents' room, just to be sure. Kristin was not in the house.

"It was her," Clint said to Hammer, who was lingering behind him in the hall. "It was Kristin." He met Hammer face-to-face. "I have to go after her."

"But . . . but . . . ," Hammer stuttered. He galloped after Clint, who was already flying down the stairs.

Clint hit the first floor. He sped through the foyer, the hall, the breakfast room, and out the sliding door.

Clint felt sweat trickle down his back. As he ran, he kept his eyes glued to the spot where Kristin had disappeared. What would he find in this part of the swamp where he'd never been? And why did it seem, as he got closer, that the wind was picking up?

Gasping, Clint finally reached the clump of grass where Kristin had gone in. Up close, he was shocked to see that it was nearly as high as his head. The blades swayed before him, teasing him. The wind made an eerie whistling as it rushed past his ears.

"Kristin!" Hammer called. He had caught up with Clint.

Yes, Clint thought. If Kristin would come out now, they wouldn't have to go in.

But there was no answer. The yellow-green spires of grass danced in front of Clint's eyes. They rustled and filled Clint's ears with a hissing sound.

Was it really the grass making the sound? Or was it the hissing of a thousand snake ghosts?

Clint shook his head to clear it. *Don't fall under their spell.* He whistled an old Amy Grant tune, "Angels Watching Over Me." He was scared, but he was encouraged too. He realized he and Hammer weren't fighting this thing by themselves after all.

The wind pushed him from behind. It was strong enough to push him a step forward. Here, even the wind fell under ghost power. It nudged him to enter the waving grass.

"You don't have to go in, Hammer." Clint still stared at the spears of grass. "But I've got to."

"Kristin!" Hammer cried again.

The sun's light dimmed. Clint looked up quickly. A cloud had floated in front of the sun. The wind gusted again. Clint's T-shirt flapped at his sides. The grass was a million green fingers beckoning him.

"I'm going in now," Clint said.

He stepped into the grass. The sound was like a million twigs cracking under his feet. *It's dry. Not a swamp here,* he thought.

The tips of the grasses pricked his cheeks. The sharp blades stroked his neck. They curled on his shoulders like many long fingers. *Woo, woo, woo,* the wind chugged past his ears.

"Clint!" Hammer yelped.

"I'm here!" Clint called. As he twisted his shoulders, the grass surrounded him with rustling. *That is just the grass rustling, isn't it?* Clint thought.

"You should have seen it! That grass just ate you up, man!"

"I'm okay," yelled Clint.

He went forward. One foot, then the other. There was no path here. Clint held his arms like a wedge, pushing the grass aside as he walked. His feet were lost in green tangles. When would he ever break through this clump? *Would* he break through it? If he did, would he be lost? "Kristin!" he yelled.

"Kristin!" Hammer's voice echoed behind him. He was trying to follow Clint. But the tall grass made it difficult to keep sight of his friend. "Keep talking, Gleeson! So I can make out where you are."

Clint's heart pounded with fear.

The wind was furious now. It whipped the grass wildly. "I see you, man!" Hammer shouted. "That's the stuff. You're blazing a trail!"

"Kristin!" Clint hollered.

The forest of tall grass came to an end. Clint was now under a canopy of tree foliage.

He continued to walk forward as he turned his head to look behind him.

That's when Clint tripped.

He began tumbling, and tumbling, and tumbling.

16

He was rolling head over heels.

Clint squeezed his eyes shut. Was he tumbling down a chute that the ghosts had dug for him? He didn't want to see its narrow walls. He didn't want to see the snakes, easing their coils along ledges, flicking their tongues at him.

He hit bottom.

For a few moments he lay there dazed.

Clint forced his eyes open.

He had landed on a mound of foliage. It had broken his fall.

He turned and looked behind and above. He had rolled down a giant hill.

He turned again and looked straight ahead. Ten yards in front of him, a tall, skinny tree rose up toward the sky. The tree was dead. Its bare branches clattered against each other in the wind.

A thick strand of poison ivy climbed and wound around the tree. The massive vine seemed to

squeeze the tree trunk like a boa constrictor squeezing its prey.

At the base of the tree a large loop of green vine
seemed to be moving. It looked like it was crawling.
It was—

A snake!

A snake just like the one from the basement.
Harmless? Out of the swamp, maybe. But what had
Hammer said? In the swamp, anything goes.

Hammer. Where was he?

Clint whirled and jerked his head up.

From above him, the voice rang down: "Gleeeeson!"

Bits of brown dirt from above rained down on
Clint. The dirt pelted his face. He turned and buried
his face in his arms.

When Clint finally looked up, Hammer was standing beside him.

"Hey, man," Hammer puffed.

The snake! Clint whirled toward the tree.

It was gone.

"Which way would Kristin go?" Hammer asked.

"Who knows?" Clint shook his head. His thoughts
were jumbled. He gazed at the greenery surround-
ing them. Except for the dead tree, the land was wild
with leaves and vines.

"She'd go where the story is," Clint murmured.

"Oh, man, you are giving me the creeps," Hammer
said. "Make sense, will you?"

"She must be at the cabin." The wind snatched Clint's words away. "That's got to be to the right."

Clint and Hammer began to trudge through the plants and bushes. Even this deep in the forest, the wind continued to whip against them. In fact, it seemed to be picking up. It blew so long and steadily that the boys had to fight to stand.

"We weren't expecting a hurricane, were we?" Hammer yelled.

"The sky was clear and sunny when we were back at the house," Clint answered.

"Well, we're in the swamp now. Anything can happen," Hammer said. "Is it my imagination, or is it getting darker?"

"I think it *is* getting darker. We've got to hurry. If a storm's blowing in we could get trapped in here."

They had only struggled a few yards past the dead tree. Clint stepped carefully. He was sure that snake was close by.

"Kristin!" Clint yelled. While he walked west, the wind blew his words south. When he called her, it was like yelling in two directions at once.

Ooooooooooh, the wind moaned through the trees.

"I didn't know wind could blow so hard," Hammer said.

Because it's not the wind, Clint thought. *It's the ghosts' breath. And whatever the ghosts want to do on this land is going down now.*

Well, I've got news for them. There's a mightier wind than this. Don't they know spirit means "wind"? When the Holy Spirit blows, they better watch out!

Up ahead Clint spotted something gauzy and white fluttering in the wind. As he got closer he suddenly stopped in his tracks, horrified by what he saw on the ground in front of him.

The wind tossed glossy blonde hair up from the ground, scattering it like corn silk.

"Oh, man," Hammer moaned.

Clint opened his mouth. But not even a croak came out.

He stumbled forward.

In front of him Kristin lay motionless on the ground.

17

"Kristin!" The name burst from Clint's lips. The grass hissed like a nest of vipers as he crouched at her side.

Her ice blue eyes stared up at him.

Clint felt tears well in his eyes. What had the ghosts done to his sister?

Kristin sat up.

Clint shuddered and jumped back. Hammer screamed.

Something about Kristin's expression looked unnatural to Clint. Now he understood. The ghosts had turned his sister into a zombie.

Clint scrambled to his feet. His legs tingled. His bones felt like sponges.

Kristin stood and took a step forward. Clint and Hammer took a step backward.

Kristin blinked her eyes. The wind whipped her hair. She looked normal now. And her wrinkled face looked very angry.

Clint scrunched up his to match. "Just what were you trying to pull? I thought you had been hurt!"

"I'm not pulling nothing." Kristin began to cry. The wind snatched at her dress. "You spoiled it again."

"What? What did I spoil?" Clint's throat felt raw. "Come on, Kristin," he rasped. He reached for her. "Don't cry. Let's go home. Maybe Mom's there."

"Nuh-uh." Kristin scrubbed at her face with both fists. She straightened her white dress and shook her blonde hair. Then she turned and ran away—farther into the swamp.

Rustling sounds filled the air and the grass all around. The boys charged ahead. But in only seconds, they had lost sight of her. They had no idea which way Kristin had gone.

Hammer stopped running.

Clint stopped too.

They had to think.

The wind was tearing leaves off the trees now. It snatched leaves from all the bushes, vines, and plants, flinging them through the air. The leaves swirled and slapped the boys' faces.

"The ghosts are ripping the joint apart," Hammer croaked.

"Yeah." The word scraped out of Clint's throat. "The ghosts are done with it."

"And with everything in it."

Clint shuddered.

"And you know what that means." Hammer's whisper was harsh. "De-struc-tion!"

Just then lightning flashed. Seconds later thunder rumbled overhead.

"The storm's here!" Hammer yelled. "Which way do we go?"

"The cabin." Clint heard the weak sounds that came out of his mouth. His throat felt as if he'd swallowed a razor blade. He sounded like a sick kitten.

"Cabin!" Clint said again. He pointed ahead to their left.

Side by side, the boys entered the darkest part of the swamp. Here the tall treetops had all grown together. The branches swayed wildly in the violent wind.

How, Clint wondered, would they ever find their way? They had never approached the cabin from this direction. And it had never been this dark.

And what if they found their way, only to discover that Kristin was not at the cabin? That she had lost *her* way?

Lightning flashed again, illuminating the ceiling of green leaves. In that instant, Clint thought he saw shadows closing in on them.

The ghosts have surrounded us!

A clap of thunder made both boys scream.

Clint was suddenly aware of something flying through the air. It struck his right shoulder and sent him stumbling into the swishing grass beyond.

18

"Hey, man." Clint, lying in the grass, heard Hammer speak. At least, he thought he'd heard Hammer. The voice sounded like bricks being dragged over rocks.

Something kicked Clint's leg. Then the weight of a body landed on him.

"Ooof. Hammer!" Clint screeched. His throat felt like it was on fire.

"Gleeson?"

"Hammer!" Clint croaked. "Did it get you too?"

"No, man. But that tree limb really smacked you good. The wind is pretty wild." Hammer put his hand to his throat. "Oh, man, I've got to stop talking."

Clint let Hammer haul him to his feet. They pressed their fingertips against bark to feel their way around trees. They brushed damp nets of low-hanging leaves out of their faces.

A low, deep rumbling sounded overhead. It seemed to shake the earth.

"If we're caught in a storm then where's the rain?" Hammer grunted.

Clint shook his head. There were no sensible answers. *That's right. This is not a storm.* So who could say the rumbling was thunder? The ghosts could be blowing up the ground under their feet.

They reached a small clearing. They could see the clouds above them.

The sky had become a ceiling of gray-black thunderheads. Then a whole network of lightning split the sky into a jigsaw puzzle. Thunder shook the boys' ears, their hearts, the whole earth. And then the rain poured down.

Clint and Hammer stood in the clearing as water poured down on them. It soaked their clothes, their shoes. Their dripping hair was plastered against their heads. Lightning flashed around them like a fireworks show. Each deafening peal of thunder made their stomachs leap. They did not dare go into the trees now.

They could only guess at what might be happening to Kristin.

Neither of the boys was wearing a watch. They had no idea how long the rain lasted. But after a while, the drops no longer ping-ping-pinged against them.

Clint looked at Hammer. His friend was as wet as

if he'd gone swimming in the Gulf with his clothes on. Hammer's black hair looked like it had been painted on.

Clint was sure he looked as bad. He gazed down at his own T-shirt and saw how it stuck to his body.

Clint and Hammer craned their necks toward the patch of sky above the clearing. The clouds were starting to break up.

The air smelled earthy. Rain trickled from leaves all around. It sounded like a million dripping faucets.

Saving his voice, Clint pointed forward.

The boys waded into the thick trees again. At once they were showered again by the drops from the leaves.

Clint's courage rose when he saw that the trees were starting to look familiar. By now he and Hammer must have crossed into the part of the swamp that they knew. The jail tree couldn't be far ahead. Then they'd only have to go down the little hill to reach the cabin.

All of a sudden Hammer scuffed to a stop. He grabbed Clint's arm and pointed at something ahead of them.

Something white, thin, and limp was snagged on a low branch just ahead. It had been soaked by the rain.

Clint knew instantly what it was.

That fine white fabric tangled in the tree was a piece of Kristin's dress.

"She got away." Hammer squeaked like a mouse.

Clint knew those words were meant for comfort. Kristin had freed herself from the tree—a tree that could have been struck by lightning.

Or maybe she did not free herself. Maybe she had been taken away. Clint banished the thought. He ran to the tree and grabbed hold of the cloth.

It was the skirt of Kristin's dress. How long and hard she must have struggled to tear off the skirt of her dress.

Clint tugged at the cloth.

The branch tugged back.

Clint seized the cloth and tried to work it loose. But the branch seemed to have countless twigs sprouting from its ends. Every one of them had burrowed its way into the dainty cloth.

"Hey, man," Hammer squeaked behind him. "Leave it. We'd better find her."

They ran now as fast as they could through the

snares of vines and the juts of uneven ground that tried to trip them. All the trees shook their leaves on them as they passed, spraying them with water. Lower clumps of leaves, like wet mops, smacked their faces.

The jail tree loomed ahead.

Pelting toward it, Clint scanned between its vines for sight of his sister.

Clint and Hammer stopped short of the jail tree. For some reason it appeared even more menacing now.

Its countless arms waved. Its countless knotholes, looking like wooden eye sockets, stared. It dared them to search it, to take their chances in its prison of vines.

Clint turned his face away.

"I've got to go in there. I think that's where Kristin is," Clint said.

"Don't, Clint. I think it would be a mistake." Hammer's face was grim.

"No, you don't. You'd do the same if it were your sister. I know you would."

Their eyes locked. What Clint said was true.

"Before I go, I just want to say that you've been my best friend ever. Don't forget that if—if something should happen."

They clasped hands for a moment and held each other's gaze. Then Clint was gone.

How long Clint was gone, he couldn't say. Once inside the tunnel, he seemed to enter a new dimension of time and space. Complete darkness engulfed him, and he took a few moments to let his eyes adjust.

No sooner had his vision accepted the darkness than he regretted his rash decision. He wasn't alone. Two eyes were looking directly into his.

20

Clint's breath became short and rapid. The beady eyes remained fixed on him. Clint didn't dare move. He and his tunnel partner were engaging in the staring contest of his life.

Soon Clint realized he could no longer hold his cramped position in the tunnel. The rains had been strong enough to penetrate the jail tree and the tunnel's mossy covering. The walls of the tunnel were damp and Clint's sweaty hands were failing to keep him in place. He knew as soon as he moved that he'd lose the contest—and who knows what else. Would he ever see his family again? Would anyone ever find Kristin?

Since he was about to fall prey to the horrible beady eyes anyway, Clint decided he had nothing to lose by striking out. With a quick prayer in his heart, Clint inhaled sharply and thrashed into the darkness, hoping to injure the eyes or some other vulnerable part of the beast's body.

He hit the eyes, all right. And he hit other soft, vulnerable body parts. In fact, the beast was nothing but softness. It was a teddy bear.

This was too strange. What on earth was a teddy bear doing in a moss-covered tunnel in the middle of a vine-covered tree in the heart of an overgrown forest?

Clint peered farther into the darkness. There were other beady eyes, other bears.

"Kristin?" Clint called softly. "Kristin, are you there?"

He pushed aside the bears and felt the wall for another passageway. One bore to the left and another to the right. He opted for the left.

This would certainly be a good time for a ball of string, Clint thought, remembering his concern for Tom Sawyer and his spelunking adventures. He could very easily become lost in the darkness and never find his way out.

"Kristin?"

Only a few feet later he came to a wooden door and tried to pull it open. It was locked. He had no choice but to back up and try the other passageway.

This tunnel led to another door, but it was partially ajar. Cool, refreshing air was drifting through. Clint was about to enter when he heard hissing sounds and laughter. The voices were drawing near.

No time to lose, Clint thought. Quickly he ducked

behind the bears clustered at the entrance to the tunnel.

His timing had been dangerous. A ghostly figure drifted past him just as he slipped out of sight. Clint didn't dare continue his search. He longed for the world of daylight and green trees.

Above ground, Hammer looked as if he'd seen a ghost himself. He had.

"Man, am I ever glad to see you!" Overjoyed, he threw his arms around Clint's neck. "When that ghoul came out of the tunnel, I was sure he'd had lunch first and that you'd been the main course. Good thing he didn't see me or I might have been dessert.

"What did you find in there?"

"What I found makes no sense, Hammer. The tunnel was packed with teddy bears! What I wanted to find wasn't there. Kristin was nowhere to be seen." He felt a lump rising in his throat.

"Don't give up, yet. There's still the cabin."

Hammer mopped his face with the tail of his wet T-shirt. But it was like trying to dry off after a swim with a towel that had fallen into the pool. "We are just about there. Right? To the cabin?"

"Nothing between us and it except this tree and a hill," said Clint. "A small hill. Downhill."

"The way things are going, it might as well be a mountain. Uphill. Is it just me, or does it feel as if we've been in here for about two weeks?"

"It's not just you," Clint said slowly.

They'd gone through a kind of night and day, with the storm. Clint began to wonder just how late it was.

Could it be that the swamp was not only slowly eating his yard? Could it also be swallowing time? How much of their lives would be eaten up here, before they finally got free?

"Come on. Let's get your sister and get out of here. If we don't find Kristin, we still get out of here. Then we go for help."

Clint and Hammer raced past the jail tree. They made it all the way to the top of the hill without anything happening. They looked down at the cabin.

Now it was the color of charred wood drenched in water. The thick brush that hulked close to it made lumpy shadows.

"Man," hissed Hammer. "If that's not the ghosts' headquarters, then they don't have any."

"A tunnel under the floor," Clint remembered out loud.

"Zillions of frogs," Hammer reminded him.

The frogs had been real. They'd seen the frogs.

Clint started down the hill. Hammer kept pace.

"We'll look in all the windows," Clint suggested. "First the side one. Then the back one straight across from the door. Then the other side one, if we need to."

Clint took a breath. The last thing he was going

to say scared him most. "If we can't see anything through the windows, we try the door."

Hammer said nothing. He was staring wide-eyed. His gaze was focused somewhere behind Clint.

Clint saw that Hammer's lips were pressed together tightly. His face, under his black hair, looked bleached. He looked as if he had seen a—ghost!

21

Clint spun around.

Racing up behind him was a soaked little girl. Her blonde hair was stringy and looked stiff as sticks. She wore a ragged white top over a regular shirt. She had on shorts where the skirt of the play dress had been torn away. She was wide-eyed. She was silent.

"Kristin!" Relief bubbled through Clint. "Are you okay?"

She didn't answer.

"Kristin? You *are* okay, right? Where were you when it was raining so hard? Did you get hurt?"

Kristin opened her mouth slowly. Then she burst into tears. "I was so scared. The thunder hurt my ears," she wailed. "And I tried to run but a big tree grabbed me. I pulled and pulled but it wouldn't let go. It tore my dress."

Clint held his little sister, patting her back until her sobbing subsided.

She sniffled and looked up at her brother. "Clinty, it's not even the right day," she said. "Did you know that?"

"What are you talking about?" Clint's voice was getting better. It was strong enough to rise above a raspy whisper.

He guessed what Kristin was talking about. Time in the swamp was much different from time in the world outside it. The longer they were trapped here, the bigger and wilder the time difference became. Somehow Kristin knew that they were now on a whole different day.

"I know how to get the right day back," Clint told her. "All we have to do is go home."

Kristin frowned as she studied her brother's face. "How is going home going to help it be the right day, Clinty?" she asked.

"Well," Clint said. "I think the day that's out there must be the right day. Because the enchanted forest is the only place where the day is different. In every other place, the time is the same. So let's just go home."

Kristin thought hard about this for a moment, then understanding lit her face. "Ooooohhh. 'Course. The 'chanted forest has different days. But that's okay. I meant it was the wrong day for me to be Goldilocks. The wrong day again. See, first it rained and I got all wet."

"Goldilocks doesn't get wet in the story?" Clint prompted. He tried to nudge Kristin toward the little hill. She didn't move.

"A tree doesn't rip her dress in the story either. I ran to the Three Bears' house to hide from the thunder." Kristin was speaking rapidly. "But when I got here, the Three Bears were home." Kristin flapped her hand toward the cabin. "And Goldilocks doesn't go in when they're home. Because that's not in the story."

"What?" Clint blinked. Slowly he reached out. He gripped Kristin's arm.

Hammer made a gurgling sound.

"Clinty, what are you doing? You're squeezing my arm."

"Three bears?" Clint loosened his grip.

"Yeah. The Three Bears are home," Kristin said. "They must be done with the porridge. 'Cause now it's sitting time. They're sitting in their chairs. One, two, three in a row. Go look, Clinty."

Clint met Hammer's eyes.

"Go look, Clinty," Kristin repeated.

Clint and Hammer ran to the cabin. It couldn't be. They couldn't see three bears on chairs. It wasn't possible.

Yet thousands of frogs appearing overnight didn't seem possible either. But he and Hammer had seen them.

The windows were streaked with dried rivers of mud from the storm. Together, the boys propped their foreheads on the glass. They cupped their hands around their eyes. They peered in.

And screamed.

In the middle of the cabin, three bears sat on a row of three chairs.

"This can't be," whimpered Hammer.

Clint felt weak. He thought he should sit down. But he couldn't. If he took his eyes off them, the bears might disappear. Or they'd turn into frogs. He had to keep standing. He had to keep looking.

It was still too dark in the cabin to see the floor clearly. Clint could not see if there was a hole in the floor leading to a tunnel.

"They look stuffed," Hammer said.

"Like the ones in the tunnel," said Clint.

"They're all the same size. No Papa, Mama, and Baby bear."

The bears did look like giant toys. The boys couldn't make out color. But the bears had to be brown or black. Around the edges they could see ratty tufts of fur.

"Even if they are only stuffed bears, what are they

doing in there? I mean, how did they get there?" Clint said.

"Just what I was thinking," Hammer whispered.

"And where are the frogs?" Clint grew more nervous as he spoke. "Hammer, this cabin was full of frogs yesterday."

"Maybe they went through the hole in the floor. Maybe they're in the tunnel now." Hammer looked at the ground beneath his feet. The frogs could be under there now. He looked back through the window.

"And maybe those are real bears and the ghosts put a spell on them to freeze them. You know, make it so they can't move." Clint didn't like how Hammer's voice buzzed against the window.

"But why would ghosts trap bears in a cabin and make them stiff as statues?"

Hammer didn't have an answer.

"Let's look around. If there is a tunnel here as well, maybe there's an entrance nearby," he finally said.

They spent some time looking around the foliage near the cabin for telltale signs of a tunnel. Perhaps there was some overgrowth blocking an entrance, maybe a tall bush that seemed out of place. It was just too hard to tell. The rain had turned everything wet and soggy.

"This isn't getting us anywhere," Clint said. "I think we should go in."

"Into the cabin?" Hammer asked, incredulous.

Clint knew what Hammer was thinking. As much danger as they were in now, it didn't compare with being inside the cabin. If there really was a ghost tunnel underneath, they were stepping directly into harm's way.

"Look, what choice do we have? You and I both know that this isn't going to stop unless we come up with the courage to do what we have to do. For some reason, you and I have seen the ghosts. Nobody else has; or at least, nobody has seen what we've seen.

"We can't very well go to the police. What do we tell them? There are teddy bears next door and a secret tunnel? You know what my parents would say if we talked to them. We have to take action while there's still time."

Clint's words hung in the air between them. Having said them, he now had to act.

"Okay, I'm going in." His feet were like lead as he moved to the door. It was one thing to say you were going to have courage and quite another to actually have it. He turned back to Hammer. "At the first sign of trouble, you grab Kristin and beat it!"

Hammer nodded solemnly and clutched her hand.

It seemed an eternity before Clint found himself at the door of the cabin. His fingers worked and his palms sweated as he contemplated the knob. There was no putting it off any longer.

He tried the knob, not knowing whether he wanted it to be locked or not.

It wasn't.

He turned it and the door swung back on its hinges.

This seemed the time for screeches and screams to come from the underground caverns. But there wasn't a sound. His trespassing had gone unnoticed. All that greeted him were three dopey-looking bears perched on chairs.

Hammer ventured to peep around the doorjamb. "Clint?"

"Come on in. The coast is clear."

Hammer cautiously entered the cabin with Kristin in tow.

"Let's look this place over thoroughly. If we find anything, we don't touch it, but we make note of anything unusual."

"Right," Hammer agreed.

Slowly they began to scour the one-room cabin. There were no signs of a tunnel beneath the table. There were no loose boards. No knotholes triggered springs that opened hidden passageways. The windows were shut tight and locked. Why the door had been unlocked they could only guess.

"This is crazy," Hammer said. "Bears coming and

going. Frogs appearing and disappearing. You and I both know there were frogs in here. And now there's no sign of them."

Clint wouldn't have heard Hammer's voice even if he'd had answers for him. Clint's attention was focused on the bears. Something strange was happening.

A bulge began to form in one arm of the bear on the right. Right below the shoulder.

"He's not a toy?" Hammer whined.

"He's sure not frozen in place," squeaked Clint.

The bulge rippled.

"Do bears have muscles that look like that?" asked Hammer. His voice rose high and stayed there.

"Bears are strong," squealed Clint. "But I don't think bears can do that."

"What about ghost bears?"

"I don't think with ghost bears there are any rules," Clint said.

"Well?"

The sharp voice behind him made Clint jump.

"Well?" the voice shrilled again. It was Kristin. "Now do you believe me about the Three Bears?"

"Yeah," Hammer croaked. Like before, he could hardly make a sound.

"Take my hand, Kristin," Clint said, without taking his eyes off the kooky bear. In his fear, Clint's voice slid up and down like a broken flute.

"But I want to see the Three Bears," she said,

pouting. She wasn't tall enough to see the strange go-ings-on, and Clint couldn't very well let her know the bears were flexing their muscles right before his and Hammer's eyes. If she got a hint that the bears were alive, she might decide they were getting ready to go on their walk.

"Not right now, Kristin. Remember, they're at home and they're not supposed to see you," Clint urged. He maneuvered her toward the door and jerked his hand in Hammer's direction, motioning for him to follow. But Hammer was mesmerized by the bears.

"The ghosts must have made these bears pump iron," Hammer chattered nervously. "Oh, man, look at that!"

Something was now happening to the bear on the left. Its stomach was beginning to bulge.

They had to get out of here, Clint knew. But his knees had turned to jelly.

At that moment a huge bump began to grow on the top of the middle bear's head.

"Nobody," Hammer panted, "but nobody, has a muscle like that on his skull."

"Look!" Clint croaked. He pointed to the bear on the right, the one with the bulging arm. A third arm was now slowly growing out of the bulge. It was just a baby arm, though. Skinny. But long. And hairless. Dark, shadowy, rubbery, it kept coming, coming—

"Snake!" cried Hammer.
At that moment the second bear's belly exploded.

23

Snakes poured out of the bear's stomach. Clint couldn't tell how many there were. He couldn't tell the head of one from the tail of another. The snakes flopped and wriggled over one another as they burst out of the mangy bear and slid down to the floor.

They wasted no more time looking for the bottomless hole. Clint picked up Kristin and ran for dear life. Hammer was right behind.

They ran for what seemed infinity before they finally came to a clearing and fell to their hands and knees, breathless.

"We . . . can't stop," Hammer wheezed. "The tunnel . . . We didn't find one . . . but . . . those snakes know where it is . . . That means they could get out of the cabin, underground. That means they could pop up . . . behind us.

"Anywhere. They could pop up just anywhere. Let's beat it," said Hammer.

Clint turned to Kristin. He was about to grab her arm and run when an eerie cackle pierced the air.

Kristin screamed and grabbed Clint around the leg.

"Run!" Hammer yelped. "Whatever it is, it's close!"

Hammer took off running. Clint grabbed Kristin's hand and began to run so fast he practically dragged her behind him.

The loud, ghostly cackle sounded again.

Clint risked a glance over his shoulder.

He caught a glimpse of something stepping out from behind one of the trees.

24

Clint didn't stop to get a better look at the strange figure. He kept running, pulling Kristin along behind him.

Hammer reached the edge of the Gleesons' yard first.

Clint and Kristin entered the yard just as Hammer was climbing onto his bike.

Gasping for breath, Hammer stammered, "I've . . . got to . . . get . . . away from here." He tried to inhale deeply. "Call me . . . later."

Panting heavily, Clint watched as his friend pedaled away.

Kristin started to cry. *She's tired and confused,* Clint thought. *For that matter, so am I.*

Clint took Kristin into the house. He went to his bedroom and threw himself on the bed, staring at the ceiling. He was still trembling.

He thought about the figure he had seen. Although he had caught only a brief glimpse, he was certain the figure was not a snake. In fact, in that split second Clint was sure he had seen a man.

Nothing made sense. Frogs that appeared overnight and then disappeared just as quickly. Stuffed bears loaded with snakes. The shrill cackle and then the figure that stepped out from behind the tree. What was *really* going on?

Clint's mind was racing.

"I need a soda," he said out loud. His throat was parched.

On his way to the kitchen, Clint passed through the family room. His mom and dad were watching the evening news.

Kristin was curled up in her dad's lap. To Clint, she appeared to be sleeping.

Clint had just stepped out of the family room when the newscaster said something that grabbed his attention. He turned back and sat down in front of the TV.

Clint rarely watched the news on television, but he found this particular report interesting. He listened intently.

When the report was over, Clint went to the kitchen and got the soda. He sat down at the snack bar and began thinking again about the experience in the swamp.

He was forming a plan.

*   *   *

After supper, Clint called Hammer and told him of his plan. It involved another trip into the swamp.

"I'm not sure, Gleeson," Hammer said. "It could be dangerous."

"Not if we stick to the plan. Meet me here tomorrow at ten o'clock."

"Okay. If you're sure this will work."

"I'm sure," Clint said. "I'm sure."

Hammer was right on time the next morning. Clint went over the plan a second time to make sure his friend understood.

"Remember, we have to stay on the path to the cabin."

"Right," Hammer said.

Hammer and Clint stepped into the tall grass at the edge of the swamp. They made their way to the path that led to the cabin.

"I sure hope we don't run into any cackling ghosts today," Hammer said loudly.

"Or any snakes," Clint replied.

They passed the jail tree and began to climb the little hill.

"Listen," Clint whispered. He stopped walking and concentrated on listening.

"What is it?" Hammer stopped alongside his friend.

"I thought I heard a voice."

Both boys strained to hear.

Suddenly the loud cackle of laughter filled the still air.

Hammer and Clint screamed simultaneously.

They looked up and saw a tall, gangly figure at the top of the hill.

"So you've come back to join usssss," hissed the figure.

The figure's skin was ghastly and pale.

Clint realized he was sweating. For a second he began to doubt his plan.

"I hope you can run fast today," the figure said as it glared at Clint and Hammer. "Because if you don't, you will stay here with usssss forever." The figure threw back its head and released another ghostly cackle.

But Clint knew this was no ghost.

"Freeze!" a voice shouted.

The figure tried to run, but someone grabbed it from behind and wrestled it to the ground.

"Good work, boys." A police officer stepped into view. Another officer, the one who had wrestled the gangly figure to the ground, now had him in handcuffs.

"Clint!" Mr. Gleeson came out from behind a clump of bushes where he had been anxiously watching the plan unfold. He rushed over to embrace his son.

"We have the second smuggler in cuffs down by the cabin," one of the officers said. "If it hadn't been for you kids, I don't think these guys would have been caught."

"That's right," another officer said. "They would have hustled out of here and moved their little game somewhere else."

"I wouldn't have thought of it if I hadn't caught that report about smugglers on the news last night," Clint said.

"When the report listed the kinds of animals smuggled—you know, poisonous frogs from South America, exotic reptiles—I got interested."

Clint wiped beads of sweat from his brow.

"And when the report said smugglers often hide the animals by sewing them into suitcase linings, or even stuffed animals, I got suspicious."

"And if somebody doesn't sew well enough," Hammer added, "*Blammo!* Snake explosion."

"The cabin was their pickup point," an officer said. "They played along with your fear that there were ghosts haunting the land.

"And it almost worked. If they had cleared out early this morning, they probably would have gotten away."

Mr. Gleeson put one arm around Clint's shoulder and the other around Hammer's. "Come on, guys. I think you heroes deserve a special lunch."

Clint looked at Hammer and smiled. They traded

high fives, then walked down the path toward the Gleesons' house.

The crowd applauded and cameras flashed as Clint, then Hammer, shook the mayor's hand. There had already been a couple of articles in the newspaper about their adventures in the swamp. Now there would be one covering their awards ceremony one year later.

"These are indeed fine examples of today's youth," the mayor intoned. "We hear a lot these days about the irresponsibility of our youth and their declining moral values, but here we have two young men who, out of concern for their community, faced their fears and overcame them."

Clint tried to tell everyone that he wasn't brave at all but that he had prayed to the Lord to protect him. He hoped his message got through. He knew without the Lord by his side, he'd have never been able to carry out his plan and crack the smuggling operation.

He knew Hammer felt the same way. He was going to youth group more often these days, and every time Clint turned around, there was Hammer reading his Bible. Hammer said he didn't believe in ghosts anymore—at least not any more than he believed in angels. He said if he had a choice he'd rather believe in them.

Clint's parents bought the property next door to their house, of course, and fixed up the cabin to rent out as a one-room bed-and-breakfast. It was really cute, and tourists often came for a few days' stay. As part of the renovation, the tunnels were filled in and the grounds were landscaped and made safe. Needless to say, the name Haunted Swamp stuck, and the boys were often called upon to recount their tales to new B&B guests.

Clint had another year of Little League to go. He still played first base, and now he wasn't distracted by the view of the "swamp." He was hoping they'd do well in the tournament this year, and by the looks of things his prayer would be answered.

Kristin no longer played Goldilocks but her hair certainly warranted the name. She was going to be in kindergarten this year. She thought a lot of her big brother and told everyone how big and strong he was.

Sometimes Clint and Hammer still retreated to the jail tree. It did turn out to be a great hideaway. They let Kristin in on the secret and she kept it close.

"Things sure have changed in the past year, haven't they, Hammer?"

"I'll say," he answered. "You know, I love the jail tree and all that . . ."

"Yes, go on," Clint said.

"And the cabin's a great place to hang out when there's nobody around . . ."

"Right . . . so why do I hear a *but* coming?" Clint asked.

"There's just one thing I don't think I'll ever get used to."

"What's that, Hammer?"

"Teddy bears. If I ever see another one as long as I live it will be too soon."

7

The mummy tumbled on top of me and pinned me to the floor. I kicked and pushed against it. "Chick, help me!" I screamed.

But my twin brother was too busy racing down the path to the front sidewalk to do me any good.

I was still struggling to get the mummy off me when, unexplainably, it began to float in the air away from my body. I couldn't believe what I was seeing. Did this mummy have mystical powers?

I swung my fist at it, but it was already out of my reach. When I tried again a voice called out, "Stop! Stop, Keri! Don't hurt the mummy."

"Dad, is that you?"

"Yes." Dad laughed. "Who else would bring a mummy into the house? This is only a replica, but it's valuable. I have to get it back to the museum. It's a replica of a male who was embalmed more than two thousand years ago," he said as he carefully leaned the mummy against the wall.

He turned and grabbed my extended hand and pulled me to my feet.

"Thanks, Dad. What time is supper? I've got a lot of homework, and I don't want to be up too late. A girl has to get her sleep before she hangs out with a bunch of old dead people in an ancient tomb," I told him.

"About five. Mom has her Red Cross safety and first-aid class after work, so she won't be joining us for supper tonight," Dad said.

He called out the door to Chick, "Come on in. Monstro won't hurt you."

"Monstro? Dad, where did you get a name like Monstro?" I laughed as I tossed my knapsack on the dining room table.

"Monstro the mummy. I thought it was cute."

"Dad, that guy is anything but cute. Maybe we should dress him in a nice sweat suit?" I suggested.

Dad grinned as Chick entered the house. They were talking as I went off to my room to wait for dinner.

Dad is a great cook, but I must have added too much salt to my food. I was parched all evening. I drank several glasses of water between dinner and bedtime.

I was still thirsty in the middle of the night and had to get up to get a drink.

The night-light in my room had burned out several

weeks earlier, so without a light I stumbled out of bed and felt my way along the hallway. It was dark, I mean *very* dark. There wasn't even any moonlight.

I took short steps and ran my hand along the wall. Suddenly, my fingers brushed against something that wasn't supposed to be there. I slowly reached out until my whole hand touched a solid object covered in gauzy material. I shuddered and snatched my hand away.

Monstro!

I took a deep breath to calm my racing heart. I had been around Egyptian artifacts all my life. I knew that a mummified human couldn't hurt me in any possible way. I was sure of it. At least, I knew I *should* be sure.

I glided my hand through the kitchen doorway and along the wall until I touched the fridge, then the countertop. I was only inches away from the sink. The glasses were kept in the cupboard above it.

When I came to the cold stainless steel sink, I raised my hand, popped open the cupboard, and grabbed a glass. I really needed a drink of water.

As I pushed the faucet handle up to release the refreshing water that my throat needed, my hand slipped.

The stream of water came out full force into my glass. It blasted into the bottom of the glass and then up the sides and out of it. The strong force of the spray drove streams of water all over my face, hands, and body.

I jumped back to avoid getting totally drenched and crashed into something. *What?*

I jumped again when I saw the shadowy form beside me. *Jesus, help me,* I prayed. I reached out my hand and instantly recoiled when it touched gauze-like material.

Monstro had followed me into the kitchen!

I stumbled backward to the sink. The hard spray of water was bouncing off the stainless steel and onto the counter, the floor, and my pajamas. It was cold, and my natural reaction was to leap forward. When I did, I slammed into Monstro.

I pushed myself off him and sailed backward into the side of the sink. I rolled to my left to avoid the icy water that was spewing out of the sink and onto the floor.

I reached over and smacked the faucet handle down to shut off the flow. That took care of one crisis. But it was the next one that concerned me most.

If Monstro was up and about and moving through our house like a living being, I had to do something. But I needed some light.

I scooted my back along the refrigerator until I came to the wall with the light switch. I flipped the switch but no light came on.

Had Monstro cut the electricity to the house?

I heard a horrible grinding sound as if Monstro was gritting his teeth to ready himself for his human meal.

My mind raced. *What should I do next? Help me think, Lord,* I thought. The grinding noise grew louder in my ears.

Then it hit me. I had flipped the switch for the garbage disposal.

I knocked that switch off and the one next to it on. I squinted against the sudden light. As my eyes adjusted, I shifted my gaze to Monstro.

I burst out laughing.

Mom's Red Cross dummy was standing in the middle of the kitchen. She must have been practicing her bandaging techniques.

I was still laughing when a hand touched my shoulder.

"Ahhh!"

"I'm sorry, Keri. I didn't mean to scare you," Mom said. Dad was standing behind her, and I could see Chick behind both of them stifling his laughter.

I looked around me at the puddle on the floor, the Red Cross dummy, and my drenched reflection in the window glass.

"I'm sorry about the mess. I just wanted a drink, and I didn't want to turn on the light and wake anyone up."

"Well, since, we're awake, we'll all help clean this up. We should be done fairly quickly," Dad said.

"Chick, I think the three of us can take care of this. Why don't you go on to bed?" Mom said.

Chick was more than glad to escape the labors of sopping up water from the floor.

We finished our work. Dad turned off the kitchen light as I was entering the door to my bedroom. The dark wasn't as frightening as it had been earlier. In my own room, I knew where everything was.

When I was little, I used to imagine things hiding in my room. One time I was sure a snake was on the back of a chair near my bed. The next morning, I saw that it was only my belt. Another time I thought I saw a ghost, but it turned out to be only my white skirt hanging on a hook in my closet.

The dark wasn't nearly so frightening now as it had been.

I yawned as I crossed the floor of my dark room. I was awfully tired. What should have been a five-minute thirst quencher had turned into a twenty-minute floor scrubbing. I was thinking how nice my warm, soft bed was going to feel.

I pulled back the covers and slipped in between them. It was definitely time to sleep. I rolled over to grab my pillow.

Instead of feeling the plumpness of my pillow, my hand touched the raggy texture of . . . ? My blood ran cold.

My arm was around Monstro the mobile mummy!

I yelled and leaped from my bed to the other side of the room in one jump. I flipped on the light.

It wasn't Monstro in my bed. It was only a bunch of cleaning rags tied around a broomstick. *Chick!*

I turned to see Chick crumpled on the floor laughing.

I laughed too. I was getting too jumpy. "Goodnight, Chick."

At school the next day, Chick and I went through the cafeteria line before heading to our favorite table where Del and Josep were saving places for us.

As I sat down I said to Del, "I am beat. That mummy that my dad brought home attacked me in the hallway, the kitchen, and then in the bed."

Del's eyes opened wide with fear.

She gulped and said, "Attacked you? How? How could it attack you? If the mummy at your house came to life, then couldn't the ones at the museum come to life too? I don't want to be a midnight martyr to a mobile mummy."

"There's nothing to fear," Chick threw in. "Except for the Curse of King Tut."

"The what?" Josep and Del spoke loudly and in unison.

"You've never heard of it?" Chick said. He turned to me and asked, "Do you think we should tell them? They might not want to camp out with us in Tut's tomb."

"Please tell us. We've got to know," Del begged.

"We've got a right to know if we will be in danger," Josep added.

"We really should tell them," Keri added.

Chick sat back in his chair. "Well, okay. But the two of you have to promise that you'll go with us anyway."

"It's a promise," Josep said. Del nodded her head in agreement.

"There is a curse on King Tut's tomb. When it was first opened they found . . ."

The bell for the next class interrupted him.

10

Del and Josep were stunned when the bell rang. They needed to know about the Curse of King Tut but couldn't be late for class. Unfortunately, there wasn't time enough to tell them.

The rest of the day went quickly, at least for me. When we stepped outside to wait for my father to pick us up, Josep and Del were waiting for us.

"We've been waiting all day. You have to tell us about the curse now," Del pleaded.

"There's not enough time to finish before Dad arrives," Chick said.

"We've got some extra time," I said. "Don't you remember? Dad said he would be about fifteen minutes late."

"Maybe you were making it all up," Josep said.

"Go ahead and start, and you can finish the story in the car on the way to the museum," Del said persuasively.

"All right. But when you're scared out of your

wits and start shaking in the middle of the night, don't blame me," Chick said.

"Chick and I read the story again last week. So we know the facts about King Tut's curse really well. Too well," I told them.

I shuddered.

"Twenty men and women were present when Howard Carter and Lord Carnarvon opened the tomb of King Tutankhamen," Chick began.

"At that time, no one knew if it would be filled with treasure or be one more pyramid that was looted by burglars.

"When the group opened the tomb they found the great treasures that you'll see tonight. The group was excited.

"Then Howard Carter found a clay tablet with hieroglyphics on it. Another member of the team, Alan Gardiner, decoded the Egyptian writing. That was when fear struck the archaeological group.

"The inscription read:
Death will slay with his wings whoever disturbs the peace of the pharaoh.

"Carter, Lord Carnarvon, and Gardiner weren't afraid of a curse, but they knew that their Egyptian workers would be. They hid the clay tablet. In fact, all mention of the discovery was taken out of the records. No photos exist because soon after it was translated, the tablet disappeared."

"So, what's so scary about that? A tablet disappeared, big deal. Sometimes my homework vanishes. That doesn't mean that there is a Curse of Josep."

"There is a lot more to the story, and it gets scary," I said. "Within two months Lord Carnarvon came down with a mysterious illness. He woke up one morning with a temperature of one hundred four degrees, but he was shaking with the chills.

"The next day, he felt better. But the day after that, the chills and fever came back again. This went on for twelve days."

Chick jumped into the story. "The twelfth night at one-fifty A.M., Carnarvon died. Moments later, all the lights in the city of Cairo went out. Even stranger, Lord Carnarvon's prize dog back in England died at the same time. The butler said that the dog began to howl, sat up on her hind legs, and fell over dead."

Chick took a deep breath. "There is more to the story. Do you want to hear it?" he asked. The two stared at him and nodded their heads yes.

"Arthur Mace was the guy who removed the last chunk of wall that blocked the entry to the main chamber. Soon after Carnarvon died, Mace complained that he was getting more and more tired with each passing day. Suddenly, he went into a coma and died. The disease was never diagnosed.

"A friend of Carnarvon, George Gould, went to Cairo after he heard about Carnarvon's death.

Howard Carter showed Gould around Tut's tomb. The next day, Gould was dead," I said.

"Then another man visited the tomb. He returned to England, but the curse followed him there. He died mysteriously of a high fever."

"Another man, Archibald Reid, cut the cords around the mummy. He grew very weak and died too." Chick added.

"Within six years, twenty-two people who helped open the tomb or who had been connected to the Tut treasure died. The strangest account involved Howard Carter's employee, Richard Bethell.

"One morning, Bethell was found dead. When the workers told Bethell's father, the father died. Then, on the way to the cemetery, the hearse ran over a little boy."

"Even the guy who wrote the Sherlock Holmes mysteries said that the curse had caused all the deaths," I added.

"Wow! Do you think that the curse is still on the treasure?" Josep asked.

"I guess we'll find out tonight," Chick replied. At that moment, our dad drove up and we jumped into the car.

Everyone was very quiet on our trip to the museum.

When we were almost there, Josep finally spoke up. "Were you two telling the truth about the King Tut curse?"

My dad turned his head toward the boys in the front seat and asked, "Have you been talking about the curse again? Did you mention the one about the mysterious deaths? Or the one about Tut walking around at night protecting it?"

Del threw herself forward in the seat. She grabbed my dad by the shoulder and asked, "Do you mean it's true?"

11

A car horn sounded behind us before Dad could answer, and about that time we turned into the driveway to the museum. Del and Josep looked at each other. They were curious, but they were also scared.

"Once we park, grab your stuff out of the trunk," Dad instructed. "Stay near me so security can clear us in one big group. Once inside, we can drop off our things by Tut's tomb."

We entered the front door and headed straight for the tomb.

We stacked our things by the entrance to the rebuilt interior of King Tut's final resting place.

We stopped in front of a large replica of the *Egyptian Book of the Dead* papyrus. Josep looked at my dad and asked, "What's that weird creature?"

Dad smiled and answered, "That is the Egyptian god Ammet. He is part crocodile, part leopard, and part hippo.

"To the left of Ammet is a set of scales. Ammet's

servants are weighing the heart of a recently deceased Egyptian. If his heart is filled with good, then he passes into the next world. If the Egyptian's heart is not filled with good, the eternal outcome is not so positive."

Chick asked, "Dad, what are these little people statues?"

"They look like the little toy soldiers and cowboys that we played with when we were kids," said Josep.

"Not exactly. Egyptians believed that when they died they would have to work in the fields of the gods. But they also believed that if these small figurines, called *ushabti,* were buried with them, then the *ushabti* would do the service for them."

Josep chimed in, "I'll have to make sure that my action-figure collection gets buried with me." The rest of us laughed at that. Being Christians, we didn't have to depend on toy soldiers to get us to heaven.

Dad walked away from the Egyptian section into the prehistoric wing of the museum. Del and I followed him. We stared up at the dinosaur bones all around us.

"Dr. Hoffman, how do they keep those things from falling apart?" Del asked. "Look how long the neck is on that dinosaur."

"Can you see the cables coming down from the ceiling? They can support a tremendous amount of weight."

"Then these are *real* dinosaur bones?" Del asked.

"That's right," Dad said.

"That is so cool. But if all we have are bones, how do we know what they looked like with skin on them?"

"We don't know for sure, Del. But we do know how muscles work. And if you lay muscles over the bones and then skin over the muscles, than it's pretty close to what you see in those pictures over there," Dad explained.

Suddenly, a scream pierced the air.

"Dr. Hoffman!"

SPINE CHILLERS™

When top science students Chick, Keri, Del, and Josep join a professor of Egyptology at the traveling pyramid exhibit, they expect to see strange signs. But some things are impossible, aren't they? The kids aren't so sure when two mummies come to life after lights-out and begin stalking them.

It's too late to go home in . . .

Tuck Me In, Mummy

SpineChillers™ #9
by Fred E. Katz